Bruce and the Mystery in the Marsh

The Bruce and Friends Series

Book 1: *Bruce and the Road to Courage*

Book 2: *Bruce and the Road to Honesty*

Book 3: *Bruce and the Road to Justice*

Book 4: *Bruce and the Mystery in the Marsh*

Other Works by Gale Leach

The Art of Pickleball: Techniques and Strategies for Everyone

Short stories and poems included in
Avondale Inkslingers: An Anthology
and
Inkslingers 2013: Memoirs of the Southwest

Visit
www.galeleach.com
to learn more about these books
and others in the works.

To an interested reader —

Bruce
and the
Mystery
in the
Marsh

by

Gale Leach

Gale Leach

TWO CATS PRESS
Surprise, AZ

Bruce and the Mystery in the Marsh

Two Cats Press
17608 W. Columbine Drive
Surprise, AZ 85388-5623

Cover design by Elizabeth Engel.
Book design by Gale Leach.

Second edition 2014
Published by Two Cats Press, Surprise, Arizona.

ISBN-13: 978-1-937083-34-2
ISBN-10: 1-937083-34-9

For Rebecca
with great affection

Acknowledgments

My husband and friend, Richard, is at the heart of my writing success. Always ready with an ear, an eye, or a hand, he keeps me going even when I can't see the words anymore. His usual advice has been shortened these days to "just keep writing." He's right.

Morgan, thank you for the keen insights and questions that improved the flow and the characterization of this book.

Elizabeth, you've created beautiful new renditions of the characters on this book cover. No easy task. Thanks for working so hard to find the way they "really" look.

Jim, thank you for teaching me to revel in good criticism, and for supplying such again with your edits to this manuscript.

Finally, thanks to you, readers and friends, who bring a purpose to these creations. Writing may be a solitary endeavor, but you're always with me in my thoughts.

Contents

Cast of Characters

(* indicates the character appeared in a previous book)

*Agatha	A praying mantis who is a Master Chef.
*Arlene	A butterfly. Bruce's mother.
*Angie	A moth. Good friend to Bruce, Milton, and Carly.
Armand	A salamander who lives not far from Cecil.
*Bruce	A butterfly and the hero of the story, which is told (mostly) from his point of view.
*Carly	A scorpion. Friend to Milton, Bruce, and Angie.
Cecil	The victim, a walking stick insect. The first master chef and Agatha's mentor.
Devon	A dung beetle. Cecil's student who discovers his body.
*Dora	An orb weaver spider. Friend to Milton, Bruce, and Angie.
Elvira	A slug and elderly neighbor to Cecil.
*Eugene	A ferret (weasel). Brother to Lilly.
Frederick	A walking stick insect. Cecil's brother.
George	A gerbil. One of Cecil's students.
Horace	A dragonfly who was Cecil's helper.
Isabelle	A salamander who aspired to master chef status.

Jemma	A jumping spider who lives in the marsh.
Kyle	A crab. Bodyguard for Armand.
*Lilly	A ferret. A past friend to Bruce, Milton, and Carly.
Lydia	A walking stick insect. Both Cecil and Frederick were in love with Lydia.
*Meryl	A mockingbird (deceased). Bruce's first real friend who died battling with Stang.
*Milton	A jumping spider and Bruce's long-time friend.
Nadine	A shrew. One of Cecil's students.
Orville	A woodchuck. A trader in goods and services.
Polly	A walking stick insect. Cecil's daughter.
Rodrigo	A walking stick insect (deceased). He and Agatha were in love before he died.
Sam	A butterfly who is traveling in the marsh.
Seymour	A beetle who is caught stealing Cecil's things.
*Stang	A bat (deceased). An evil fruit bat who terrorized other bats into doing his bidding.
Tanya	A shrew. Nadine's mother.
Vivian	A salamander. Armand's cousin.

Chapter 1

The Death Is Discovered

"Agatha! The Master Chef is dead! I think he was murdered!" The dragonfly flitted from side to side, and his beating wings caused bits of dust to fly around Agatha, who stood at the entrance of her home in the willow tree.

"Whatever are you talking about, Horace? Calm down," Agatha said. "*I'm* the Master Chef!"

"Not *you,*" Horace said, panting. "The first Master Chef—Cecil. He's dead!"

Bruce and his mother, Arlene, who were visiting, appeared behind Agatha.

"Horace, come inside and explain all of this properly."

The dragonfly shook his head, puffing to regain his breath. "Can't do that. Have to spread the word. Lots of chefs to tell."

"COME IN!" Agatha bellowed.

The dragonfly's wings stopped beating for a

moment, and he fell, landing with a plop on the ground. Even Bruce and Arlene cowered a little and moved a step back from the praying mantis, Agatha, who was obviously agitated.

"All right, all right! You don't have to shout," Horace said, as he straightened his wings and composed himself.

Agatha relaxed a bit and said, "Come here and explain what happened. I'll give you some tea."

Looking a bit less upset, Horace started to shake his head again, but evidently thought better of it. "Well, just a little. I can't stay long. Have to spread the word."

He flew up and flitted inside the opening, followed by the two butterflies, Arlene and Bruce, and finally Agatha, who set about preparing the tea.

"All right," the mantis said. "Now start over and explain what happened."

The dragonfly took a deep breath. "Some time ago, Cecil—"

"Cecil Thornberry, the first master chef and my mentor," Agatha said to Arlene and Bruce.

Horace frowned at the interruption. "As I was saying, Cecil asked me to stay with him. He was getting old, and he found it hard to get around. He wanted my help with errands and cleaning. In return, he said he would teach me how to become a chef."

Arlene returned from her cooking area carrying a small tray loaded with cups of tea. She set the tray down and placed one cup near the dragonfly, who sipped it.

"Oh, that's hot, but it's good. Thank you," Horace said, taking another sip.

"I can't believe Cecil is gone," Agatha said, her eyes misting over. "He won the first five cooking competitions, you know. Everyone said his cooking was the finest they'd ever tasted. I was in awe of him after I decided to become a chef. One day he took me aside and offered to teach me what he knew. By that time, he'd retired from the competitions, but he was always there, watching and commenting about what the chefs were doing. One of his comments actually helped me win the first time I entered."

"How did that happen?" Bruce asked.

Agatha opened her mouth to reply, but the dragonfly interrupted. "Agatha, I can't stay all day."

Agatha's face darkened in a scowl. "Horace—how did Cecil die?"

The dragonfly looked so upset, Bruce thought he might cry. "I don't know. When I came this morning, and I found him—I was so bothered seeing Cecil just lying there. I saw a note on his desk—it talked about murder. I came straight to you because you always know what to do at times like this."

At the word "murder," Agatha looked a bit ruffled. "I'm glad you did. You were always good to Cecil. He couldn't have asked for a better assistant." She took a deep breath and let it out in a sigh.

"It's not the trip I planned to take, but I need to get to the bottom of this. I owe Cecil that much and more."

"Agatha, I'm sorry to have brought this sad news," Horace said, taking a last sip of tea. "I must be going. I want to let others know about Cecil, too."

Agatha shook her head. "No, Horace—don't do that. In fact, we must keep this quiet until I can get there and examine the scene. I'd like you to return to Cecil's home and keep everyone outside, away from his body, until I arrive. Make sure nothing is disturbed."

The dragonfly nodded as he walked to the doorway. "All right. You'll come soon?"

"Yes. Thank you, Horace," Agatha said, as he zoomed away. Turning to Bruce and his mother, she said, "Horace is a little slow sometimes, but he's a good sort all the same. He doesn't always get the facts straight, though, so I won't know for sure what happened to Cecil until I get there." She spread her wings a bit and ruffled them before laying them back down again—a trait which Bruce recognized as a sign of her nervousness. "Arlene—I've enjoyed having you and Bruce here. I don't like ending our visit early, but I must."

"Agatha, I'm so sorry," Bruce's mother said. "Cecil must have meant a lot to you."

"I can't believe he's gone," Agatha said. "I had planned a trip to see him again soon, and now it's too late." She sighed.

"I would go with you," Arlene said, "but I must get back home to tend to the nectar we harvested. Another few days and it will be too late." She regarded Bruce and twitched one of her feelers. "I know you were eager to help us store the nectar," she said with a smirk.

Bruce turned red. Ever since he'd been old enough to help, he'd always tried to find an excuse to keep him from assisting with that particular chore. When he was a very young caterpillar, he offered the thought that he was too small, but his mother found tasks he could do. When he grew larger, he said he had homework, but that didn't work, either. Now that he'd become a butterfly, Bruce knew he was stuck.

His mother continued, "However, you worked hard with the harvest this season. I think we can manage on our own. Why don't you go with Agatha and make sure she gets there safely?"

Chapter 2

Off with Agatha

Bruce couldn't believe what he'd heard, and he lifted his wings high, hoping to convince Agatha to take him along before his mother changed her mind. He wasn't particularly excited to see a dead chef, whatever kind of creature he might be, but it had to be better than dealing with all that sticky, gooey nectar. "May I go with you, Agatha? I'll be good company."

Agatha smiled. "Better company with me than groaning with your mother while you finish the nectar? I'd think so." She winked at Arlene. "Of course you may come, and Milton's tree is on the way, I believe. He'd be welcome, too, just like old times."

"That would be great!" Bruce said, but then his face fell. "I just remembered. Milton may still be visiting the orb weaver spiders. Would we be going in that direction?"

"I'm afraid not. Cecil lives—" She paused, looking stricken. "I mean, lived—in the marsh, not far from the docks where you got on the ship to go to the cooking competition on the island. In the days when Cecil was my mentor, I lived much closer than I do now."

"Do you still have family there?"

"Yes. But families of mantises don't stay together like yours do. Mantises have a habit of eating each other, you know. Our family reunions would be grizzly affairs at best."

Bruce's eyes widened, and he thought back to his first adventure. He'd run away from home because the other caterpillars teased and bullied him. He hadn't wanted to change into a butterfly because he was afraid of heights and had no desire to fly. He'd met some new friends, and all of them agreed not to eat each other. In time, their group included a mockingbird, a jumping spider, a firefly, a moth caterpillar, and others, including Agatha. They had traveled to a cooking competition where the insects and animals abided by that same code. He didn't worry about getting eaten when he was with them. He was still careful when he flew from place to place, however. Just as when he'd been a caterpillar, he knew that great numbers of other birds, insects, and reptiles loved to eat butterflies.

"Probably better if we don't go there, then," Bruce said, smiling. "So Cecil was a praying mantis, like you?"

"No. He's a walking stick." Agatha paused again, looking at her teacup. "Or, rather, he *was* a walking stick. If you haven't ever seen one, I wouldn't be surprised. Most creatures miss them completely, because they look just like twigs."

"You said Cecil was your mentor? He taught you how to cook?"

"I knew how to cook," Agatha said. "Cecil taught me to be a *chef*. I spent many days with him, while he taught me how to use spices properly and how to make food look appealing. I learned about new types of food I hadn't heard of before—foods from other parts of the forest and from distant deserts, where they have ingredients that don't grow here. He and I traveled quite a lot, experimenting with new foods and combining them in new ways. He also taught me a great deal about other uses for herbs and ingredients, such as poultices and medicines."

Agatha was animated now, thinking about times gone by. Her eyes twinkled. "I enjoyed those days immensely, and Cecil always encouraged me, although he allowed no foolishness. I worked very hard, but it was fun." Agatha's smile faded a little. "I'm going to miss him very much. I'll be glad to have you along with me to say goodbye—and Milton, too, if we find him at home."

"Agatha—" Bruce thought about how to ask his question without upsetting the mantis. "Horace, the dragonfly who was here, said something about murder. Do you think Cecil was murdered?"

"I don't know, Bruce. I hope to find out. Then I'll know what to do."

"What do you mean?"

"If I discover he *was* murdered, I intend to find out who killed him."

"And when you figure that out?"

Agatha's eyes flashed. "I'll make sure he gets what he deserves."

It was a quick departure. Arlene gathered her things, hugged Bruce, and even hugged Agatha—a difficult task, but they managed it as best they could.

"When I get back, Arlene, and this is settled, I'll come your way and we can talk more about your entering the cooking competition," Agatha said.

"Don't worry about that," Bruce's mother said, as she headed outside. "Do what you need to do. I'll see you both soon! Bruce—be careful! Watch out for—"

"I'll be fine, Mom," Bruce said, wondering if he would ever be old enough that his mother wouldn't think of him as a tiny caterpillar any more.

Arlene lifted her wings and caught a draft that took her upward. Bruce watched her go, as she flew close to the trees and the bushes that had sweet nectar to sustain her along the way. He hoped she would be safe, too.

Bruce had only his backpack with him—the one his mother had remade so that it fitted his new, slender body—so there wasn't much for him to prepare. Agatha brought out her large satchel and loaded it with food, herbs, spices, containers, and assorted tools Bruce didn't recognize. She bustled about, muttering to herself, and finally closed the satchel and hefted it onto her shoulder.

"This bag is heavy," Agatha said, "but I have no idea what we'll need. I'd rather be prepared with too much than find I didn't bring something and wish I had. Besides, if I get tired of holding it, you'll carry it for me, won't you?"

Bruce's head snapped around and his eyes grew large. He stared at the huge satchel and then at Agatha, only to find her grinning and realized she was teasing. It took him by surprise, as he'd never known Agatha to tease about anything before. He liked it.

"Of course! No problem," he said with a grin.

They both laughed, and Bruce thought the sad situation made the humor feel even more welcome.

Chapter 3

Milton

Once they'd started out, they made good time getting to Milton's new tree home. Bruce couldn't believe how quickly his wings took him from place to place compared to when he was a caterpillar and had to crawl everywhere. His first taste of flying had been a long time ago, when he met Meryl, his first friend, after running away from home. Meryl was a mockingbird who didn't like to eat bugs. She'd been teased and bullied as much as Bruce had, and having that in common was their first step to becoming good friends.

After that, they'd met more companions, including Milton, the jumping spider, and Angie, a beautiful moth caterpillar. Then Angie was abducted by a bat, and Bruce was determined to rescue her. Meryl suggested he fly on her back so they could get to the bat cave sooner. Despite feeling terrified, Bruce climbed up and finally grew accustomed to flying.

A hint of sadness overcame Bruce as he thought about Meryl, who died while saving him from Stang, the leader of the evil bats who took Angie captive in the first place. Bruce knew he would never stop missing Meryl. He wondered if Agatha felt the same way about Cecil.

He didn't fly as fast as Meryl used to because his wings were much smaller than hers. Still, because of her, he was able to enjoy being a butterfly, and he never regretted changing.

Bruce navigated toward Milton's tree without any trouble, even though things looked very different from the air than they had from the ground. As he got closer, Bruce knew they were in the right area because he spotted large webs glistening in the sunlight. Agatha ran and hopped along the ground for the most part. Bruce knew her satchel was much heavier than she was used to carrying. He couldn't imagine why she'd brought all the things she had, but she certainly should be prepared for whatever might be waiting when they arrived at Cecil's home.

"I see webs," Agatha said. "Be careful you don't get caught."

"I see them, too," Bruce said, even as he veered around the first one. He spotted Milton in the distance spinning a web. He was surprised to see Dora there, in a web of her own. Bruce noted that Milton's web looked very nice. Dora had taught him well.

Bruce flew very quietly and landed on a branch behind Milton, careful not to make a sound. Just as Milton was about to tie a strand together in the center of the web, Bruce shouted, "BAT!"

Milton tumbled forward into the web, as Bruce giggled. Milton waved his legs this way and that, getting completely stuck to the glistening lines. The more Milton struggled, the more Bruce laughed, until he lost his footing on the branch and fluttered to the ground. He leaned against a rock, laughing until his sides hurt.

Milton had stopped moving and hung upside down from the strands. "All right, all right. You've had your fun. Get me out of here!"

"Actually, I think you look rather handsome in that beautiful web," Dora said, "or at least it was beautiful before you became its first victim." She giggled, while Milton glowered. Then Dora's smile turned into a wicked grin. "Perhaps *I* should come and set you free?"

Bruce knew this was a bad idea. Dora was an orb weaver spider they'd met on their first adventure. It was one thing for Dora to teach Milton how to spin a web from a distance. But to have her get close to Milton … no. Just as Agatha's family tended to eat one another, so female spiders often ate their mates, as well as other spiders who got caught in their webs. While he didn't think Dora would give in to her desires and threaten Milton, he wasn't taking any chances.

"That's all right, Dora. Agatha and I will help this clumsy guy," Bruce said, as he lifted off the ground and flew toward his friend.

He and Agatha set to work snipping the web strands. This was so much like the first time Bruce met Milton that he thought of Meryl again. Agatha was not like Meryl, but she had become a good friend, too. He hoped Milton would be able to join them on this trip and that the two of them could assist with Agatha's investigation.

When they cut the last strand, Milton scowled.

Bruce ignored the look. "You know, the last time I helped free you from a web, you told me you were in my debt and must repay me. I assume that applies again?"

"Not in the least," Milton said, unable to hide his smile any longer. "It was my own clumsiness that caused me to get caught in my web the first time. This time I was ambushed, and by my best friend, too. Sad state of affairs when your best friend can't be trusted."

Suddenly, Milton leaped from the web toward Bruce. He calculated the jump perfectly so that Bruce would think he was going to collide with him on the branch, but at the last moment, he somersaulted and landed on the tree trunk instead.

Bruce let out a squeal and lifted into the air, flapping his wings as fast as he could. Milton laughed so hard, he almost fell from the tree. Bruce made a rude noise and fluttered to a branch near his friend.

"Well, are you coming with us or not? No evil bats this time, but Agatha's on a quest, and I'm helping her."

"Oh, a quest!" said Dora, who peered at them from her web above. "I enjoyed helping with your last quest, you know. If you need assistance again, come and ask me, all right?"

Milton nodded in her direction, starting to pull small bits of web from his furry legs. "Dora's expert teaching has gotten me about as far as I can go with web spinning anyway." He waved a foreleg and bowed to the large orb weaver, who saluted in return. Turning back to Bruce and Agatha, he said, "Of course, I'll go with you. When do we leave?"

One strand was still stuck to Milton's head, and it made Bruce giggle to see it dangling between his eyes. "We're waiting on you."

"Well, then," Milton said, as he leaped from the branch to the ground and landed neatly at Agatha's feet, "lead on."

Chapter 4

On the Way

Bruce was excited. Although the occasion of their going was a sad one, he couldn't help but feel something more was going to happen. He watched Milton, who had gone ahead and was waiting for them to catch up, swaying from side to side. Bruce knew Milton was excited, too.

It had been quite a while since their last adventure. Milton had remained with him for a long time after he changed, and Bruce loved having him there, although things had been different between them. They couldn't wrestle any longer, as that might damage Bruce's wings. However, when Bruce was on the ground or sipping nectar from a flower, Milton still enjoyed sneaking up behind Bruce and pouncing, landing right next to him and scaring him. This had been a favorite game for some time. Bruce was glad he'd had a chance to turn the tables on his friend this time. He also knew Milton would return the favor soon.

Bruce hadn't really thought about how different his life would be once he became a butterfly, because he never planned on becoming one. When he was young, the prospect of becoming a butterfly had scared him so much that he would simply put the thought out of his mind. Consequently, he'd never asked questions of his parents, such as what it's like to sip nectar, whether you get hungry without eating leaves, where your legs go—things like that. Now he was having to learn all kinds of little things about his new life: which flowers had good-tasting nectar, how to gather pollen, what to do if you got caught in a strong wind, and more. But he was a fast learner, and he'd found the new tastes of nectars and pollens to be very enjoyable. Not only that, it was a food that he and Milton could share, something he liked very much.

They had gone quite a way when Agatha said, "It's nearly sundown. Perhaps we should camp here and get some dinner before it gets too dark."

Bruce glanced at Milton, whose many eyes reflected the rays of the setting sun. Bruce was suddenly consumed with a great rush of affection for the spider. They had been in so many situations together, always watching out for each other, always friends. Bruce couldn't imagine a friend more different than he was, nor one who could be better. It would be good to be out together again.

But despite the similarities to their original trip, Bruce realized he'd changed. He'd grown up, and in more ways than just losing his legs and gaining wings. Now he was aware of the things that could happen to his friends and family, as well as to himself. That gave him a moment of doubt about the journey, thinking of the dangers that had happened before and wondering what might befall them this time.

Bruce gazed toward the sunset, which had bloomed into deep crimson and orange. He glanced back at Milton and smiled, but a nagging uncertainty was still there.

Chapter 5

The Scene of the Crime

Despite Bruce's doubts, they made it to the marsh by late morning without any serious problems. Once, they'd hidden after Milton heard something. It turned out to be a fox chasing a vole. Another time, they heard men in the distance and changed their route to avoid them.

Agatha said Cecil lived in a fallen tree that would be easy to find because its branches and roots now stuck up into the air the way its trunk used to. Bruce realized the tree wasn't completely dead. That meant some of its roots must still be underground.

As they got closer, Horace flew into view. The dragonfly buzzed closer and hovered in front of them.

"Thank goodness you're here. I've had a terrible time trying to keep the other animals and insects away from him. I'm only a dragonfly, you know. I'm not suited to fending off creatures larger than

I am. You wouldn't think so many other creatures would find a dead body interesting, but apparently they do." Horace flitted close to Agatha, who had a pained expression. "Oh, I'm sorry, Agatha. I hope I didn't upset you, but it's true. Oh, and quite a few others have come by to pay their respects. Cecil's daughter, Polly, and his brother, Frederick, were both here, along with many of the other chefs. I don't know how they found out about it, but apparently everyone knows. I've seen gerbils, finches, shrews, rats, wasps, grasshoppers, spiders, snakes, cicadas, bees, lizards, salamanders, toads, a turtle, a chameleon ..."

"I appreciate your diligence in guarding the remains," Agatha said, cutting off the winged creature's tirade. "Before we go in, tell me when you last saw Cecil alive."

"I checked in with him before I went home yesterday, a little before sundown. He was fine then. It must have happened sometime between sundown and early morning, when poor little Devon—he's Cecil's first student—found him this way."

"Thank you, Horace. Now, if we may have a look?"

The dragonfly flitted sideways, making room at the entrance for Agatha to pass. "The letter Cecil was writing is on his desk."

"Thank you, Horace. We'll look at that."

"I'll stay out here," he said, with a sniffle. "It bothers me to see him this way."

"I know. We'll be out soon."

Bruce hadn't ever seen a walking stick, and he wondered how large Cecil's hole in the log would be. Then he realized that if Agatha could fit inside, neither he or Milton would have trouble getting in. Agatha disappeared into the hole.

Bruce landed on one of the nearby branches and looked at Milton. He suddenly realized he wasn't eager to come close to a dead body. A shiver ran through his wings. He motioned toward the opening, indicating Milton should go first. "After you."

"Oh, no," Milton said, shaking his head. "After you. I insist."

Agatha's voice carried from inside the log. "You two stop that and come in here. I could use your help."

Bruce glided down just outside the opening. It was dark inside the passageway, and he walked forward slowly, letting his eyes adjust to the blackness within the hollow tree. He smelled burned wood and ash and realized that the tree must have been struck by lightning, which is probably why it fell.

He felt more than saw Milton behind him. Following a curving wall of wood with the tips of his wings, he rounded a bend and emerged into a large open area. The space had been outfitted nicely: a table on one side of the room was covered with utensils and bowls; in one corner at the back of the room was the cooking area, with a fireplace and an oven; and on the other side was Cecil's sleeping area, with a bed made of woven reeds stuffed with cattail down.

Yet Bruce didn't see any of that right away. His eyes were locked on the motionless body lying in the middle of the floor.

It looked just like a collection of twigs had fallen to the ground. Bruce didn't think he had ever seen a walking stick insect before, but after seeing Cecil, he realized he might have seen many without knowing it. He thought their ability to blend into their surroundings must be superb.

Agatha had plenty of room to move around, as Cecil had been even larger than she was. His body was probably half again as long as hers, and his legs, now bent close to his body, were at least as long.

Bruce had seen a dead body before. The father of one of his classmates had died not long ago, and Bruce had gone to see the body before it was buried. Somehow, this felt different. Perhaps because they were in his house and it seemed more personal.

"Come here, please, but don't touch anything unless I tell you to," Agatha said, motioning for Bruce and Milton to join her near Cecil's body. "Look at this."

He moved closer and stared at Cecil's head.

"Do you see that his head is quite a bit more red than the rest of him? If it's what I think it is, poor Cecil *was* murdered."

"How do you know?" Milton asked, backing away from the body.

"I don't know for certain, but I believe so. Milton, would you fetch my satchel?"

Milton jumped over to Agatha's bag, which was on the ground near the entrance to the room. The satchel was half as large as he was. He struggled to lift it and, groaning, eventually hoisted it onto his back. He staggered back to where Agatha and Bruce were discussing Cecil's body. He dropped the satchel behind Agatha with a thud, and Agatha jumped, flapping her wings. The resulting breeze knocked Bruce off his feet, almost causing him to fall on top of Cecil. When Agatha and Bruce regained their composure, they glared at the spider, who held up his front two legs, looking abashed.

Bruce's antennas swirled in circles as he studied the body again. "Who would want to murder Cecil?"

"I don't know," Agatha said. "There are probably some who didn't like him beating them in the early cooking competitions, I suppose. Sheer jealousy of his incredible cooking prowess might have been a reason. He was a fabulous chef. Agatha looked around the room. ""I really don't know much about what Cecil was doing lately," she said, "but I guess I'm going to find out."

"What do you mean?" Milton asked.

"If Cecil was murdered, I need to discover who did it, and I want you to help me."

The spider bounced up and down, obviously excited. "How will we do that?"

"We'll ask questions and take notes and see if we can piece together what Cecil was doing recently and find out if anyone had a reason to want him dead."

Bruce, who loved puzzles, was getting excited now, too. "What will you do if we figure that out?"

Agatha raised her forefoot, pointing directly at Bruce. "I'll make sure he gets all that's coming to him!"

Chapter 6

Searching for Clues

"Start by looking through Cecil's belongings," Agatha said, pointing to the different corners of Cecil's room. "Each of you start in a different place. Milton—why don't you search some of the cubbyholes where Cecil kept his kitchen tools and other implements. Bruce—examine Cecil's shelves with his personal things. I'll look through the papers and books on Cecil's desk."

"What are we looking for exactly?" Milton asked.

"I don't know. We just need to hope something turns up that will give us a clue."

Bruce searched, but everything he'd found so far was ordinary. He kept turning around to look at the body, expecting Cecil to wake up and demand to know what they were doing in his home. There was something creepy about looking through somebody's belongings when his dead body lay in the middle of the room.

He watched Agatha walk around Cecil's body several times, looking at him from different angles, and she kept bending down to examine some part of him more closely. Finally, she knelt on the floor and peered at the ground around his body. When she stood up, she looked at Bruce. "Find anything?"

"Not yet. Some history books and story books, and a lot of cookbooks. A collection of pretty stones. Stuff like that. Did you find something?"

"Besides the note Horace mentioned, nothing much out of the ordinary. The papers on his desk are mostly recipes and notes about cooking. Milton—how about you?"

"Nothing strange around his cooking area. Pots and fireplace tools, wood for the fire—things you'd expect. I haven't—wait." Milton reached into the fireplace and pulled out a small scrap of paper. Much of it had burned, leaving charred edges, but Milton brought the remaining piece to Agatha. Bruce moved closer to see it.

The scrap was covered with a flowing script. "Looks like part of a letter, I think," Milton said.

"Let me see." Agatha took the scrap from Milton and held it closer to the light coming in from the ceiling where she could see it better. "Most of it has been burned away, but yes, it appears to be a letter." She handed the scrap back to Milton and walked to her satchel. She dug within the contents and produced something circular that was flat and hard and completely transparent. Taking the paper back from Milton, she held the circle close to it. "My eyes are not what they used to be. I found this one day, and it has been a marvelous treasure as it makes things look bigger. Bruce, fly up here and take a look."

Bruce fluttered upward, landed on Agatha's shoulder, and peered through the circular item. He was amazed to see that the words on the paper appeared to be twice their original size. "A lot of it is charred, so you can only read a few words. Those say, 'I'm sorry ...' I can't read the next line ... then ' I won't let you go ...' and another break. '... waiting for you' ... ' At your place—I'll wait ...' 're-entering the competition ...'" Suddenly, Bruce lifted his wings, flew to the desk, and landed on one of Cecil's notebooks. He shuddered. "The last word I could read said 'poison.'"

Agatha lowered the scrap of paper. "Milton—are you sure there are no more pieces of this letter in the fireplace?"

Milton crawled back into the fireplace and searched around it. "Yes. Nothing else. Just a lot of ashes and charred sticks." He crawled back out and wiped the tips of his legs on the floor, as he swayed from side to side. "I wonder why Cecil burned the letter?"

"We can't assume Cecil burned it," Agatha said, "although he may have. Whoever killed him might have tried to hide something that would incriminate him or her. In the case of this letter, I think it was written by a female because the writing is curvy, the kind of thing many females do."

"So whoever wrote the letter killed Cecil?" Bruce asked.

Agatha tipped her head sideways as she often did when she was thinking. "That's possible, especially since the letter uses the word 'poison.' But other possibilities exist, too. We need to check into all of them before making a hasty decision."

"What about the letter Horace mentioned? The one talking about murder?"

Agatha pointed to a neatly written note on the desk. "It is addressed to the Cooking Competition Commissioner."

Bruce glided over and examined it.

"What does it say?" Milton asked.

"It reads:

Dear Commissioner Marquez,

It pains me greatly to share with you information that came as a great shock to me. While visiting friends a few moons ago, an associate of mine overheard a neighbor, one of our own chefs, admit to the theft of another chef's cookbook. Having no proof, I said nothing about it then.

During the most recent small competition, however, I realized that the recipe supposedly created by this same chef was, in fact, Rodrigo's own. Yes, it was Chef Rodrigo's cookbook that was stolen.

I ask that you ban this chef from further participation in future cooking competitions, small or large.

It is also my belief that this same chef is most likely responsible for Rodrigo's death. I lack proof of this yet, but I will continue to look into it as I can. The chef I

"And that's where it ends, followed by a squiggle." Bruce looked up from the note. "It almost seems like Cecil might have died while writing this."

Agatha nodded. "I think so, too." She walked toward Cecil's bed, surveyed the items on the side table, and scanned the other areas of the room she hadn't searched. Bruce thought she might be trying to contain her emotions, as he had seen the sadness in her eyes.

She wandered back to the desk. "If the creature who killed Rodrigo found out that Cecil was onto him or her—or would be soon—that would be a reason to kill him: to make sure he didn't tell anyone else."

Agatha walked to Cecil's cooking area and leaned over to sniff the contents of the items there. She also picked up and smelled many of the containers around the cooking pots. Finally she sniffed the stew that sat in a cauldron.

"Ah. As I suspected. It wasn't poison, although the effects are similar. Whoever killed Cecil used peanut oil," Agatha said. "Cecil was horribly allergic to peanuts and took great pains to make sure he never came in contact with them in any way. Someone added peanut oil to this stew. I can smell it." Agatha shook her head. "Poor, poor Cecil. Who would want to murder you?"

Chapter 7

Letters and a Suspect

They continued their search through the rest of Cecil's belongings, but nothing they found seemed helpful with their investigation.

Milton and Bruce searched again for anything that might be out of place or something that might have been left by whoever killed him.

In the drawer of Cecil's desk, Agatha found a notebook with a roster of his students, the days when they had lessons, and lists of things to do. A stack of papers, tied with a string, seemed to be a book Cecil was writing about the marsh and its history. Agatha also found a letter from the Commissioner of the cooking competition replying to Cecil's desire to rejoin the competition.

"I'm surprised that, after all this time, Cecil decided to take part in the competitions again," Agatha said. "Some time ago, he told me it was a competition for younger creatures, indicating he was too old to take part any longer. The fact that he wanted to start competing again seems strange."

When they'd been through everything in the room at least twice, Agatha said they'd searched enough. She repacked the circular magnifier in her satchel and placed the small fragment of the burned letter and Cecil's letter to the competition commissioner into the notebook, and put that and the manuscript about the marsh in the satchel, too.

"What are we going to do now?" Bruce said.

"Not we but I. *I'm* going to talk to everyone I can find who knew Cecil or who had recent dealings with him," Agatha said. "I'll ask them questions and try to get to the bottom of this. You two are going back home."

Bruce started to object when Milton spoke. "What if nobody knows anything?"

"Somebody knows something. The killer is out there, and he or she knows what happened. Hiding a lie is hard. It's hard to keep from sharing facts that will give you away. It's also hard to do things without being seen by someone. If I ask enough different creatures enough questions, I believe I'll discover facts that will put me on the right path."

Milton swayed from side to side. "Isn't it dangerous? What if the killer finds out you're looking for him?"

Agatha nodded. "Yes, it could be dangerous," she said. "I don't plan on letting anything happen to me, though. If it looks like I could be in trouble,

I'll stop the search and find another way."

Bruce thought about what Agatha had said. He'd been in enough danger before to know what being scared of dying felt like—wondering if you'd ever get back home again, wondering if your friends were all right. And yet—there was something exciting about the idea of chasing after this killer and making sure he—or she—would pay for having taken Cecil's life. It wasn't right that someone should do such a terrible thing and get away with it. He also didn't think it was right for Agatha to search for the killer alone. Staying together made them safer, and he also thought the three of them would have a better chance of making sense of the information they might find than one of them would alone.

"I think we should stay together. I know we're young, but we're old enough to make our own decisions. I'm a butterfly now—not a caterpillar anymore. Milton and I should stay and help with this investigation. Right, Milton?"

Milton nodded in agreement.

Agatha regarded both of them, and a smile caught the corners of her mouth. "I didn't think it would be easy to dissuade you from staying with me. I know how stubborn you are, and this proves it. When I asked you along, I didn't really think we'd be trying to solve a murder, but here we are. We can do a bit more searching now, but then I need to get back to my students. I didn't intend to be away from home now, and I have students coming in the next few days. Once their lessons are over, I can come back and search more."

Bruce nodded.

Agatha picked up her satchel and started to head outside when Bruce heard a noise. He flew in front of Agatha, motioning for her to move back into the shadows. He sped to the ceiling and hung there, upside down, with his wings flat against the ceiling of the log.

A large beetle waddled in through the opening and up to Cecil's body, where he stopped. After gazing at Cecil for a few moments, he moved to the cubbyholes where Cecil kept his cooking tools and recipes. The beetle stood on his hind legs and stretched to reach inside the cubbies. He took out several different things, and when he was loaded down, the beetle turned to go back outside. Before he could leave, Milton sailed through the air and landed on top of him, knocking him backward onto the ground and scattering all he'd been carrying. Milton pinned the beetle upside down, with his legs flailing in the air. Agatha strode forward, and Bruce flew down from the ceiling.

"Let me go! Get off of me! Who are you?"

"I don't think you're in any position to be asking questions," Agatha said, poking the pointed tip of her foreleg at the beetle, who became quite still.

"Please, don't eat me," the beetle said, his voice quavering to match the shaking of his body. "I'll bring you lots of good things to eat—I know where there are lots of bugs. Please, let me go. I'll do anything!"

"What's your name?" Agatha asked.

"Seymour."

"Why did you come here and what were you planning to do with thee things you were stealing?" Agatha asked.

"I wasn't stealing," the beetle said. "Not *really*, anyway. I mean, he's dead. You can't steal something from someone who's dead, can you? Besides, it was only small things. And I saw someone else taking stuff, so I didn't think a little more would matter."

"Who did you see, and when?" Bruce asked, as Milton kept the beetle pinned to the ground.

"A gerbil. Earlier this morning."

"Did you see what he took? What else can you tell us?"

"I don't know anything else. It looked like he took cooking stuff—you know, bowls and spoons—and a book, but it was too far away for me to see. I don't know who he was or where he went. Really, I don't know anything!"

The beetle struggled, trying to get up. Milton held him fast and said, "How do we know you aren't the one who poisoned Cecil? Maybe that's why you showed up now, knowing Cecil would have died from the poison, and it would be safe to come and steal his things."

"I didn't kill him!"

Chapter 8

Record Keeping

Agatha pulled her foreleg away and motioned for Milton to let the beetle get to his feet. "I believe him when he says he didn't kill Cecil. Peanut allergy acts very quickly, and whoever did it would have known that and waited for Cecil to die. There would have been no reason for him not to take whatever he wanted at that time—he wouldn't have needed to come back. I think this little beetle is just a common thief."

"Yes, yes! Yes, just a thief—nothing more," the beetle said, creeping toward the outside.

"It's odd when confessing to thievery is the best of possible options," Agatha said. "We'll let you go, but before we do, answer Bruce's question. What else can you tell us about the gerbil?"

The beetle stopped. "Nothing. I never saw him before. What does a bug know from gerbils?"

Milton joined the conversation. "No special markings or coloration? Anything that might help us find him?"

The beetle said, "No," but then he shifted from foot to foot and looked upward, tapping one foot on the ground. "Wait, I do remember. He was brown and had a white spot on his side. I remember because the spot looked like a mushroom."

Agatha motioned toward the outside. "Go on. Get out of here. Don't come around again."

The beetle scurried out the opening and all was quiet.

Agatha collected the cooking tools the beetle had dropped. As she put them away, she said, "So we know someone put peanut oil in Cecil's stew. That means whoever killed him knew Cecil quite well—or at least well enough to know about his allergy."

Bruce said, "We also know a brown gerbil with a mushroom-shaped white spot came here and took some of Cecil's things, including a book."

Milton tapped one of his forelegs on the ground. "That must have happened between the time Cecil died and Horace arrived."

"Not necessarily," Bruce said. "The gerbil might be our killer. It's also possible that Cecil gave those things to the gerbil, or he came and took them after Horace left to go to Agatha's."

Agatha nodded. "Good reasoning, both of you. You're thinking like detectives now. Keep it up and I have no doubt we'll find whoever did this in no time. That's important, because clues get cold very quickly."

Milton continued to bounce. "What do you mean, 'get cold'?"

Agatha finished putting the last spoon in one of the cubbyholes. "The longer it takes to ask questions, the more creatures will tend to forget what they saw or heard, and the more difficult it will become to solve the crime. So let's go over the rest of the facts we know now. Oh, before I forget. Which of you will be the record keeper? It's important to write down the evidence and what it suggests."

Bruce and Milton glanced at each other, and Milton raised a foreleg. "I'll do it. At least the words will be spelled correctly."

Bruce folded his wings and bumped against the spider. "If I write it, someone might be able to read it instead of having to decipher your scribbles."

"You shall write the clues," Agatha said, pointing at Bruce. She pulled Cecil's journal from her bag and gave it to Bruce. "Milton will check them. Let's go over what we know again. I believe that the portion of the letter found in the fireplace was from a female. What else can you figure out about that letter?"

After a short silence, Milton spoke. "It sounds like Cecil didn't want to see her anymore, and she didn't like that. Maybe she and Cecil had a relationship and he decided to break it off."

Bruce nodded. "I think so, especially since Cecil burned the letter. It would seem he didn't want to hear from her anymore."

Agatha smiled. "Yes. But what about the specific things in the letter?"

Bruce thought for a moment. "'Re-entering the competition' could mean Cecil's decision to compete again."

"Excellent!" Agatha said. "And the part about 'poison'?"

Bruce didn't reply, so Milton said, "Cecil died of an allergic reaction, not poison, so I don't think that part of the letter has anything to do with the murder. It could mean lots of things."

Agatha nodded again. "True. Anything else? Other clues we haven't discussed?"

Milton and Bruce were both quiet.

"The next step is to make a thorough search of the area outside, and you two can begin asking questions of those who live nearby after I go home. Bruce—bring one of Cecil's smaller notebooks and something to write with. Milton—your eyes are the best, so I'm putting you on tracking detail. Let's go look around the outside of this log to see if there's any other evidence."

Chapter 9

Searching Outside

The three of them split up outside, searching for anything unusual. Milton studied the tracks that led to and from Cecil's log. He accounted for their own footsteps, of course—Agatha's back feet left short, straight tracks, while the tracks made by her front feet had small serrations on both sides. It was easy to tell hers apart from anyone else's. Bruce's feet left small round indentations in the dirt, as did his own, but his were larger. The beetle's prints were like a small version of Agatha's, and Milton could see where the beetle had walked up to the log and gone in and where he'd left. Neither Milton nor Bruce knew for sure what a gerbil's footprint looked like, but they supposed the mouse-like prints were probably his. There were several other sets of footprints which Bruce drew in the notebook. Some of them crossed each other, and some had been ruined when others walked over them. When he finished, Bruce had three sets of unidentified prints.

Bruce set the notebook down and looked at Agatha. "We can't know for sure if any of these footprints belonged to the killer. Some of them might even have been made by Cecil himself. I was just thinking—the killer could have flown into Cecil's home, leaving no prints at all."

"You're right, Bruce, but it's important to check out all possible leads. If you've finished with the tracks, I've found something interesting up here."

Bruce flew to the top of the log and settled on one of the branches. Milton bounded up and landed right beside him, scaring him as usual.

"Now's not the time to do that!" Bruce said, scowling, trying to regain his composure.

Milton looked abashed. "There's always time to have fun," he said. "Even now."

Bruce scowled and made a sniffing noise. "This is serious business."

"It *is* serious," Agatha said, but she smiled at Milton. "That doesn't mean you can't be lighthearted, too. Cecil wouldn't want us to be sad. That's what I tell myself when I feel that way." She patted Milton's shoulder. "Anyway, look at this." She pointed to some seed husks in a little pile. "If I'm not mistaken, those are sunflower seed shells. Have you seen any sunflowers growing around here?"

Bruce and Milton shook their heads.

"I didn't think so," Agatha said. "In fact, I don't believe sunflowers grow in a marsh. These must have been brought from somewhere else. The question is what animals or insects eat sunflower seeds?"

"A creature would have to be pretty large to carry all of those here," Bruce said, looking at the size of the pile. "And what was someone doing up here eating them? Whatever it was must have been here for quite a while."

"Maybe it was more than one creature. They must've had some way to carry the seeds in order to bring this many here," Milton said, looking smug.

Bruce shook his head. "Don't you think Cecil might have kept sunflower seeds in his cooking area? Someone could have brought them out here and eaten them."

"Yes, that's possible," Agatha said. "Good reasoning, Bruce."

Bruce beamed, and Milton nudged him, knocking him off balance.

Agatha chuckled and climbed down from the tree. "I think we've done about all we can here. I have to be home before mid-day tomorrow—my students will start lessons at noon—so we should pack up and get on our way."

"But what about the clues getting cold?" Bruce said.

"You're right, Bruce," Agatha said, snapping her satchel closed, "and for that reason among others, I wish I could stay. I owe Cecil that much and more. However, I have responsibilities to my students, too, and they're alive, while poor Cecil isn't. I don't plan to give up finding out who did this. I just can't continue the investigation here and now."

"But *we* could." Milton's eyes sparkled, and he swayed from side to side. "We could keep searching for clues and asking questions. Then, when we find out something, we'll send Horace to tell you."

"That's a great idea!" Bruce said, beaming. "I like looking for clues and information. It's like a puzzle, and all you need to do is find the pieces and put them together. This can be our new quest!"

Agatha's feelers waved back and forth and her expression became serious. "You're treating this like a game, but it's not. The process of solving a murder *is* like solving a puzzle, but it's no game. There's a killer out there who is dangerous. If that killer learns you're investigating Cecil's death, it could be dangerous for you."

Bruce regarded Milton, who stopped swaying. Agatha was right. He felt badly that he'd forgotten the dangers involved. Still, she'd said that clues become cold quickly, and he didn't think it would be that dangerous if he and Milton just asked questions. Besides, they were both older now, and they'd been on two different adventures before, and they'd managed to get out of terrible situations in the past. They could do this. Bruce was sure of it.

"If Milton agrees, I'd like to continue searching for whoever did this. We'll be careful."

Milton nodded and bounced up and down.

Agatha closed her eyes and appeared to be thinking. Finally she opened her eyes and sighed. "All right. You've proven you understand how to investigate for clues and to reason through the evidence to arrive at possible explanations. I want you only to ask questions of the neighbors in the nearby area. Send Horace to report back to me when you have finished gathering their information. But don't go exploring, and don't start following other leads."

"But ..."

"No buts. I don't want either of you in danger. I'll come back as soon as I can." She started to pick up her satchel, but she set it down again and said, "I have it! Will you do something for me? Get Carly to help you. She'll be a full-grown scorpion now, and the poison in her stinger could be a useful asset, should you get into trouble. I'd feel much better if you'd do that. Will you, please?"

Bruce realized they weren't far from the home Carly had chosen for herself after they returned from their last adventure. He thought having Carly with them would be good, even though she had a disturbing way of saying exactly what she thought. Bruce looked at Milton, who nodded.

"Okay, we'll ask her. But even if she can't come, I want to keep looking," Bruce said, and Milton nodded again. Bruce gazed back toward Cecil's log. "Shouldn't we bury him or something?"

"Not until we have solved his murder. His body may provide more clues in time." Agatha looked up at the sun. "I must leave you to your search. Be sure to record your findings, no matter how small, and send Horace to see me if you find anything you think I should know. Horace lives just down the road, and I'm sure he'll be willing to help, but I must be going—I won't get back in time if I don't leave now. Good luck!" Agatha lifted off the ground and flew away. "And be careful!" she called over her shoulder. "Promise me you will! You'll do fine."

Bruce and Milton watched until she flew out of sight. "I certainly hope so," Bruce mumbled to himself, suddenly not so sure he trusted his sleuthing abilities as much as Agatha did.

Milton pounced on a mosquito that landed nearby. When he'd finished eating it, he said, "So what do we do now?"

"The first thing is to go get Carly," Bruce said. "Then we'll start asking questions. I just hope Carly doesn't do ... well ... what she always does." Bruce looked pained.

"She has a way of seeing inside you, and I know you don't like that," Milton said, poking Bruce, "but what she says is usually true."

Bruce bumped him back and made a face. "Yeah, I know."

"It'll be fine. I'm sure she's grown up a lot since we saw her last, just like we have. Who knows? Maybe you and she will get along just fine now."

Bruce thought about how Carly used to make him crazy sometimes on their previous adventures.

She had a way of seeing the world in black and white that was hard to deal with. She was always calling him on things he did, like the time he fibbed and she caught him doing it. She asked him why he lied. When he tried to explain that there's a difference between telling a white lie and really lying, she didn't understand. It was frustrating dealing with her, but Milton was right. Maybe she'd grown up no, and it would be different.

As he thought more about the scorpion, he realized that even if she was just the same, it would be good having her along. She had saved everyone a couple of times, and she'd gone through a lot to help Angie and Agatha and the others when they were in trouble. Odd as it was, Carly was family.

Chapter 10

Angie and Carly

Getting to the place where Carly lived didn't take long. Bruce was continually amazed at how quickly he traveled from one place to another compared to the time it used to take when he was a caterpillar. Now, it was easy for him to keep pace with Milton, who jumped and bounded from rock to bush to tree. One time, Milton even had to ask Bruce to stop and rest.

"Ha ha, you're getting old!" Bruce said.

"No, I'm not. I didn't want to stop, because I knew you would start saying things like that." Milton huffed and puffed, trying to get his breath after going much further than he normally would without stopping. It looked like he was doing push-ups as his body bounced up and down with each breath. "It's not fair. You've got a brand-new pair of wings, and I have the same old legs. Besides, you're breathing hard, too. You can hardly keep your wings up, you're so tired."

Bruce would never admit that he was winded. He glided down from the bush where he'd stopped and landed on the ground next to Milton. Turning his back to the spider, he fanned his wings open and closed, trying to send a breeze in Milton's direction. "Poor, poor spider," he said, as Milton lunged for him. Bruce dodged the spider's forelegs and lifted into the air. "Ha ha! Now I'm faster than you are, too!"

Milton frowned as he sat on a small rock beneath the bush. He raised his forelegs in the air toward Bruce. "Perhaps you are at that. Well, if anyone had to best me, I'd most want it to be you."

Bruce felt sorry, thinking his teasing had made Milton sad. As he set down next to a rock, Bruce looked at his feet, thinking how he might cheer his friend again, when suddenly Milton was on top of him, pinning him to the ground. "Don't get any ideas about how old you think I am," he said, as Bruce struggled to get free. "Tell me I'm the handsomest spider you ever saw and I'll let you up."

A voice from behind startled both of them. Milton jumped up, releasing Bruce, and both stood ready to face whoever might wish to harm them. "You are the handsomest spider I ever saw," Carly said, scuttling out from behind the trunk of a small tree. "Of course I haven't seen that many spiders, so I don't have much to gauge it by. You could be pretty darned ugly, and I wouldn't know the difference."

"Well, don't go looking at any other spiders, because none of them are going to match up to me," Milton said, bowing to Carly. "Good to see you! You've grown."

"Yeah, I'm about as big as I'm going to get. Want to see my stinger?" Carly asked, grinning.

Bruce shuddered, thinking about the poison residing in the bulb behind the pointed barb at the end of her tail. Wickedly sharp, her stinger looked like it could do a lot of damage.

"Think we'll pass," Bruce said, walking closer to the scorpion, "but it's good to know you're doing well." He raised his forefoot and touched it to Carly's claw. "Actually, it's because of your stinger that we came. We're trying to solve a murder with Agatha, and it could get dangerous. Having you along would make us feel safer. Not happier, but safer." He grinned.

Carly flicked her tail and made a face at him. She was completely brown now and quite large. If Bruce didn't know her, he would've been terrified by her large claws and potent stinger.

Carly's face became serious. "A murder? Who was killed?"

"No one you know, or at least I don't think so. A walking stick named Cecil, who was Agatha's mentor. He was a chef who lived in the marsh by the docks. When Agatha went to pay her respects, she discovered he'd been murdered, and she asked us to help solve the crime."

"Where's Agatha?"

"She had to go back home for a while because she has students coming for lessons. We're going back to the marsh to look for clues and interview suspects until she returns. So—will you come with us?"

"I'll come, too," called a familiar voice from behind them. As Angie flew into view, Bruce felt himself getting fuzzy and warm again, the way he always did when she was around.

Angie had become a beautiful moth. Her brown wings had orange edges, with large eye spots on her back wings and small spots on the front. Bruce smiled at her, blushing just a little, even though he tried hard to hold his feelings back. Despite the fact that he and Angie couldn't mate because she was a moth and he was a butterfly, that didn't stop his feelings for her.

"Angie!" Milton said, somersaulting in the air. "You look beautiful!"

Angie blushed a bit. "Thank you," she said. "I love my new wings. Bruce, don't you love flying now?"

Bruce nodded, and he wished his tongue didn't get so tied whenever he was with her. "What are you doing here?"

"I came to visit Carly. It had been a long time, and I wondered how she was doing. Actually, I planned to visit you and Milton after I left here."

"Well, at least Bruce, anyway," Milton said, smiling, and Angie became redder still.

"So where is this marsh?" Angie asked.

Bruce frowned. "Are you sure you want to come with us? Agatha says it could be dangerous. We really only came to get Carly."

Angie gave Bruce a sharp look. "Well, if you don't want me to come with you, I guess I understand." Angie threw her head back, feigning hurt, sniffing as if she were going to cry. Bruce knew she was only pretending, but her trick worked anyway.

"Of course, you can come," Bruce said. "It's just that I don't want you to get hurt."

"And you don't care about what happens to me," Carly said. "Yeah, okay. I see how it is."

"Oh, you both know what I mean!" Bruce said, stamping his feet.

Carly raised a claw and Angie touched it with one of her forefeet. "I guess we'll both be going with you, then," Angie said. "Besides, I think Carly and I will be much better at analyzing clues and getting suspects to talk than you two would."

Milton tapped his foot on the ground and nodded. "She has a point. I'd much rather talk to them than I would to you. They're much prettier."

Bruce looked frazzled, but he resigned himself to the fact that now they were group of four.

"So tell us more about this murder. What do you know so far?" Carly asked.

Bruce opened his notebook. "Cecil—that's the name of the walking stick who died. He used to be Agatha's mentor, and he was allergic to peanuts.

He died after eating a dish of his own stew which contained peanut oil. Agatha said he would never have had peanut oil in his home, so he couldn't have put it in by mistake. She said the killer must have known Cecil well, since he or she knew about Cecil's peanut allergy."

"So whoever killed him brought the peanut oil and put it into Cecil's stew?" Carly said.

Milton nodded. "That's right."

"We found some papers on Cecil's desk," Bruce said, removing one from the notebook. "This is a letter that was addressed to the Cooking Competition Commissioner. In it, Cecil says he thinks he knows who killed another chef some time ago. That chef, a mantis named Rodrigo, was found dead, drowned in the river. Those who looked into Rodrigo's death were never sure if it was an accident or murder. Some even said Rodrigo drowned himself. Agatha said she never believed that—she was sure he was killed. Cecil didn't get so far as to list the name, but he said the same chef probably killed Rodrigo, too. His very last words are, 'The chef I' and then a squiggle," Bruce said.

Angie's feelers showed her agitation. "I think Cecil's murderer might have killed him while he was writing this," she said.

"That's what we thought, too," Bruce said.

Carly shook her head. "If that were true, why would he leave this note behind? Wouldn't he get rid of it or take it with him?"

"Hmm, you're right," Angie said.

Bruce put Cecil's letter back into the notebook and said, "Then there's this letter Milton found. Agatha said the writing looks like it was done by a female." He pulled out the burned letter fragment and Angie and Carly moved closer to see it.

After she'd read through it, Angie said, "The parts that say, 'I'm sorry,' 'I won't let you go,' 'waiting for you'—those sound like someone who wanted to get back together with Cecil in a relationship." Angie scratched her head. "I don't know about the last word 'poisoned,' though."

"The fact that Cecil burned the letter might mean he wasn't interested in whoever wrote it," Milton said, "or that he was angry. Maybe she wanted the relationship, but he didn't."

Carly snapped her claws together. "If that's so, she could have burned it to hide the evidence."

The group was silent for a few moments while Bruce read through his list in the notebook. "The other clues we found are three unidentified tracks and a pile of sunflower seed shells outside Cecil's home. Oh, and the fact that sunflowers don't grow near there."

"Yes, but Cecil could have brought those seeds here from far away, and someone could have taken them from his home and eaten them outside," Carly said.

Milton smiled. "That's just what Bruce said. You're good at this already. Agatha said it was like solving a puzzle. I think with the four of us, we'll be able to figure out who did it in no time."

Looking satisfied with herself, Carly clicked her claws again, and Angie fluttered into the air. "What are we waiting for?" Angie said. "We have a murderer to catch."

Chapter 11

Elvira

The four of them followed the route back to Cecil's log where they met Horace, who was still guarding the scene. He said he was eager to help them and that it would take his mind off of the recent events. Milton and Bruce showed Carly and Angie the pot of stew, Cecil's desk, and, of course, Cecil's decomposing body. The four of them again scanned the inside of Cecil's home, making sure they hadn't missed anything in their earlier search. Finally, they went outside, where Bruce showed Angie and Carly the pile of sunflower seed shells.

Bruce opened Cecil's notebook and inspected the notes he'd written. *I guess it's my notebook now,* he thought to himself, *but it has quite a different purpose than Cecil intended*. He sighed, closed the notebook, and sat on a rock. "We don't have a lot to go on, do we? What do we do first?"

Milton looked around. "Agatha said we should

talk with the other residents of the marsh. One of them may have seen something that might help us figure this out. But I don't see anyone else around here. Do you?"

"That's because you're not looking very hard," said a voice across the path.

Everyone turned to look where the voice had come from.

"I still don't see you," Bruce said, straining to see who was talking.

A slug raised the top portion of her body from the ground and waved her antennas.

"I'm here," she said. "It's a good thing you didn't see me right away. I'm supposed to blend in, you know. Camouflage and all that. My name's Elvira."

Milton spoke first. "May I come closer, Elvira? I'm not going to hurt you."

"Of course," she said. "I know you won't eat me because of my slick. Tell that scorpion not to come any closer, however."

Carly seemed miffed. "I wouldn't eat you, anyway. You look too old to be tasty."

Elvira shook her head, keeping an eye on Carly.

Milton smiled. "We learned about 'slick' from another friend of ours, a snail, a long time ago," he said, as he jumped over the path and landed near the slug. At the same time, Bruce picked up his notebook and flew to the ground near her. Angie followed, while Carly stayed behind.

Elvira's eyestalks angled back toward Milton. "Who are you? Did you know Cecil?"

"No, we didn't know him, but our friend, the praying mantis, did."

"Horace told me Cecil died. I'm sorry to hear that. Cecil was a friend—in fact, the two of us were the last ones left from the old marsh gang. Ever since Armand arrived, everything changed. But that's another story. Horace said Cecil may have been murdered?"

"It's possible," Bruce said, trying to sound official, his wings fluttering. "We'd like to ask you some questions. Did you see anyone here in the last two days who was out of the ordinary?"

The slug's eye stalks waved slowly, and she seemed to be thinking. "Yes, there's been a lot of activity. Let's see. The day before yesterday, Armand arrived early in the morning, and he and Cecil argued. I couldn't hear everything they said because they were inside the log, but their voices were loud enough to wake me up. I assumed Armand was trying to get Cecil to move again."

"Who's Armand?" Bruce asked.

"Armand Marden. He's a no-good salamander who wants to own all the land in the marsh. He already got several other residents to move, using his threats and such. Not me! I stood up to him and told him I'm not leaving. I was born here, and I'm going to die here!"

Angie spoke up. "So you think they were arguing about Cecil not wanting to leave?"

"Probably. Cecil disliked Armand as much as I do. I know that Armand threatened him once before, but that old walking stick was smart. He said he'd written a note explaining that, if he died mysteriously, it was probably Armand who killed him. I believe he sent the note to his daughter for safe keeping. Armand left him alone for a while after that."

Bruce wrote this information in his journal as Milton stepped forward and continued the questioning. "How long was Armand with Cecil?"

"Oh, only a short while."

"Was he carrying anything when he arrived?"

Elvira's eye stalks waved again. "I can't recall, for certain. My memory isn't what it used to be." Eyeing Carly with a sour look, she said, "I'm *old*, you know."

"Where does Armand live?" Milton asked.

"On this side of the river under a large rock." Elvira slid the upper half of her body up against a tree root. "I think Armand might have killed Cecil. He wanted Cecil's land, just as he wants mine, but he won't get it. I won't give it up!"

Milton took a step back from the slug, who seemed upset.

Angie continued the questioning. "Elvira, what happened after that? Did you see anyone else?"

"Yes, of course. The normal number of students came for lessons and left, and then another walking stick arrived. I couldn't see well enough to know who it was. There was more yelling then, and the walking stick left shortly thereafter."

"You'd never seen the other walking stick before?"

"It might have been his daughter, Polly. She comes here now and again. Could also have been his brother—what's his name? Frederick, I think."

Bruce stopped writing. "Did Cecil fight with everyone?"

The slug slanted her eyestalks toward Bruce and settled back down on the ground. "Not usually. Cecil was rather mild-mannered. Lately, however, there were more arguments."

"Did anyone else arrive that day?" Angie asked, and Bruce went back to writing.

"Let's see. Armand visited again in the early evening. At first, I thought it wasn't him, and my eyes were playing tricks on me. My eyesight isn't as good as it used to be, you know. When I was a young slug, I could see well in the dark, but—"

"Elvira—" Milton prodded. "About Armand's visit?

"Yes, well, they didn't yell at each other then. Not like they had in the morning. It wasn't long after he arrived that Armand slithered away."

"Did you see anyone else?"

"There were other visitors yesterday. Before Horace came, one of Cecil's students arrived as usual, but he ran out almost as soon as he got there. I'm sure now that he must have seen Cecil's body.

Horace got here not long after, and he flew away quickly, too. A large mouse came after that, before you and the mantis arrived. When he left, he was carrying many things. My guess is, he stole some of Cecil's belongings."

"Anything else?" Milton asked.

Elvira's eyestalks circled as she thought. "Nope. That's all."

Bruce put his notebook down. "You've been a great help, Elvira. If we think of anything else and want to ask you more questions, we'll be back."

"I hope you find out who did this terrible thing."

Bruce waved to Elvira, as he and the others headed back toward Cecil's log.

Chapter 12

Following the Clues

Bruce closed his notebook. "So now we need to find this salamander, Armand. Elvira said he lives near the river under a large rock."

Milton nodded. "We should also talk with Cecil's students. One of them might be the killer, or they may know something that would help us locate him."

"You can't be sure the killer is a *him,*" Carly said, her eyes twinkling. "Females are quite capable of murdering others, you know."

Angie smiled as Bruce got flustered again. "That's so," Bruce said. He opened his notebook on top of a flat rock and urged the others to come closer.

"Let's go over where we are so far, and then we can figure out what to do next. Someone Cecil knew intentionally put peanut oil into a dish Cecil was cooking for dinner, and Cecil died because of his allergy to peanuts. This was a murder—not an accident. Elvira said a salamander named Armand visited Cecil in the morning on the day he died, so it's possible he could have put the peanut oil into Cecil's dish at that time. However, Elvira's eyesight isn't too good—she mistook a gerbil for a mouse—so we can't be sure her information is reliable. She also said another walking stick visited that day—possibly Cecil's brother Frederick or his daughter Polly—so they are possible suspects, too, depending on how long Cecil was cooking his meal."

"We also have some unidentified footprints," Milton said, "and the fact that a gerbil took some things away with him."

Bruce shut his notebook. "I suggest we start by talking with Armand. After that, we can locate Cecil's students, any of whom might have known of Cecil's peanut allergy. Then we can interview his brother and daughter, followed by other chefs who live in this area. Let's hope we get some good information from some of them."

Milton stopped his swaying and appeared concerned. "But Agatha said we shouldn't leave this area until she got back. If one of the creatures we question is the killer, won't they become more dangerous if they know we're asking questions and trying to locate him?"

Bruce thought for a moment and said, "That's true. But there's no other way to get the information. If we wait too long, the clues will get cold. Agatha said that, too."

"Whatever we do, we need to stick together," Carly said. "It will be a lot harder for the killer to do us harm that way. 'There's safety in numbers,' my mama always said."

"I'd have liked to have known your mother," Milton said, smiling at Carly.

Bruce surveyed his companions. "Shall we go find Armand?"

Everyone agreed, although Bruce still had a nagging feeling that they were probably walking into trouble.

They started down the path that led toward the river. The marsh was different from anything Bruce had ever seen. Some places were completely flooded, and the trees and reeds and grasses that grew there looked like they had no roots. Other areas were mushy, muddy spots, like small islands that weren't large or high enough to ever dry out completely. Some of the area didn't get a lot of sun, since large trees blocked the light.

Overall, they found the going to be fairly easy. Bruce and Angie flew above the path, while Milton and Carly made their way along the drier areas, skirting pools and puddles of water. Some of the reeds and cattails that bordered the path were so high, they seemed like small forests by themselves.

Several times they stopped and took cover when they heard the sounds of predators. The hoot of an owl sent Carly and Milton scurrying behind a rock, while Angie and Bruce clung closely to the bark of a tree, hoping to blend in and not be seen. Another time they heard birds chittering as they flew by, headed toward an open area of the marsh. Taking cover beneath the leaves of a bush just off the path, Bruce again thought about the many dangers he and his friends faced, if not from the killer they were pursuing, then from those who would make them their next meal.

They had only gone a short way past a small pool by the side of the path when something pink shot up in front of Bruce as he flew by. As quickly as the pink had appeared, it returned in the opposite direction with Angie attached. Before Bruce could react, he saw Angie's entire body, wings and all, disappear into the mouth of a huge frog sitting in that pool.

Bruce wheeled in the air and headed for the frog. Without thinking about what he was doing, he smacked his shoulder into the frog's nose. Pain erupted in Bruce's shoulder and neck, but the frog didn't budge. Bruce flew backward and prepared to do it again. Before he could, though, Milton and Carly were there. In a movement almost too quick to see, Carly whipped her tail back and then lashed it forward so the stinger penetrated the frog's side.

The frog screeched in pain. Milton leaped to the frog's open mouth and spread his legs to keep the frog's jaws apart. Carly stood on her back legs and grabbed the frog's lower lip and tongue with one pincer. With the other pincer, she reached into the frog's mouth and pulled Angie out and onto the ground.

Angie sputtered and gasped. She looked terrible, completely covered with a wet, gooey fluid, but at least she was alive. Bruce's terror subsided a bit, but he found he was trembling. Milton jumped away from the frog's mouth, and Carly released her grip on the frog's lips and tongue. The frog fell over and lay still.

"Is he dead?" Bruce asked.

Carly shook her head. "No. I stunned him, though. He'll sleep for a while, and he'll have a headache when he wakes up."

Bruce helped Angie walk to the small pool of water. He rinsed her wings and washed the gooey liquid from her body and legs. In a different circumstance, he might have felt embarrassed, but now it was simply necessary to get her back to being normal again.

When the last trace of goo was gone, Angie fluttered her wings for a long time until they dried. When she finally stopped fluttering, Bruce gave her a hug. She started to cry then, and she sobbed for a little while as Bruce held her. When she had cried her fill, she dried her eyes and looked at her friends.

"You saved my life," she said. "When I saw the frog's tongue coming for me, I knew I was dead. Then you reached in to get me, and … I couldn't believe it, Carly. I still don't believe it."

"Thank Milton, too," Carly said. "He kept the frog's mouth open."

"How come the frog didn't die?" Bruce asked. "I thought when you stung things, that was it."

"No," Carly said. "It depends on how much venom I inject. I can choose to use just a little or a lot. In this case, I didn't think it was right to kill the frog just because he was hunting for lunch. I just didn't want him to have *this* lunch."

Bruce smiled and shook his head. "Angie, we've done some amazing things on our adventures together, but I think getting yourself swallowed by a frog and living to tell about it is high on the list. I only hope we're not trying to outdo each other for who can die the grossest death and come back to tell about it."

Angie smiled, which was what Bruce had hoped would happen. She hugged each friend in turn. "No competition from me," she said. "If I never see another frog, it will be too soon."

Milton surveyed the path ahead of them. "We probably should keep going. It may be a little while before we get to Armand's house, and when we finish talking with him, we have a long way back. I'll lead."

Bruce moved closer to Angie and said, "Stay close to me, okay?"

Angie looked at Bruce and smiled. "With pleasure," she said.

Chapter 13

In the Marsh

"You didn't tell me we'd have to wade through a bog," Carly said, trying to keep her head above the soggy weeds and moss. "What happened to the path?" As she raised her legs out of the soupy mush, Bruce saw they were covered with the slippery remnants of green and brown plants that had wilted and decayed.

They had traveled quite a while without any incidents, and the going had been relatively easy. Now they'd reached a place where the path had simply disappeared beneath a watery layer of wilted leaves, grasses, and mud.

"Carly's right. You two have it easy," Milton said, pointing upward with a leg also covered in muck. "You can just fly over this stuff."

Bruce watched as his friend jumped from plant to plant, trying to avoid the mushy bog that nearly covered Carly. She wasn't able to hop like Milton and had to forge her way through it. Bruce flew ahead until he came to a spot where the bog ended. A drier area led to a small, mossy plain that was beautiful and lush, in many shades of light green. He flew back and said, "You'll be out of the muck soon," pointing ahead toward the moss. "Follow me."

When Carly and Milton reached the drier area, Bruce laughed. Carly looked like a shaggy, dark green scorpion. She began removing the soggy plants that were stuck to her legs and body, and Angie helped by pulling bits and pieces of the muck from her back and tail. Bruce did the same for Milton, dragging away some long strands of gooey grasses that trailed from his back.

Looking much more like a scorpion now, Carly headed to the mossy area. "Ah, this is better," she said. "Like walking on fuzz."

Milton bounded to a tree that overhung the moss and jumped down. Without warning, the moss gave way beneath him, and he began to sink. Murky, dark ooze quickly covered him as he scrambled, trying to regain a foothold on the moss above. The more he struggled, the farther down he went. In only instants he'd sunk up to his eyes in the stuff.

Angie cried out. "Bruce! Milton's sinking!"

Before Bruce could turn around, Carly plunged into the muck after Milton.

Bruce flew back and looked around, but he saw nothing. "Angie—where's Milton?" Looking around, he realized Carly wasn't anywhere to be seen, either. "Carly? Where are you?"

Angie flew over the spot where she had seen them last. "Here!" she said, her voice shrill.

A bubble emerged from the ooze where Angie pointed, and Bruce spotted the tip of Carly's claw. Then it, too, was gone. He hunted for something he could use to push into the mud and reach to his friends, but the only things nearby were a few tufts of tall grasses.

Angie had seen the grasses, too, and she flew to one of the long stalks with a seed head at the top.

"Bruce! Come help me push this stalk down." Holding onto the stalk, she flew so the seed head leaned over the spot where their friends had gone under. Bruce landed on the stalk and helped her keep it bent over, as Angie pressed the seed head down through the surface.

"Carly! Milton! Reach up!" Angie called, hoping her friends could hear her through the mud.

Nothing happened. Another few bubbles appeared, but nothing moved. Bruce feared the worst.

"Oh, Bruce—we're losing them!" Angie cried, and she pressed the seed head deeper into the ooze. Bruce was afraid she might also get stuck if she pushed any harder.

"Milton! Carly! Reach up above you!" Bruce yelled. "Grab hold of the grass!"

Suddenly, the stalk quivered and sank deeper into the muck. Angie's legs and body followed with it and were now covered in gooey moss. She and Bruce both let go of the stalk and Bruce pulled Angie backward away from the moss. Bruce's spirits rose, thinking that either Carly or Milton had taken hold of the grass.

"Angie, help me pull it back!" Bruce flew to the middle of the stalk, grabbed it, and flapped his wings hard. Angie did the same. Together they pulled the stalk backward slightly, away from the hole, only to have the grass jerked from their grasp again. Then Bruce saw one of Carly's pincers rise from the ooze and clamp onto the stalk as she dragged herself upward.

Carly struggled, pulling with one large claw and then the other, until her body was nearly out of the muck and her middle legs scrambled on the moss. Finally her back legs were out, and she lay on the green surface, panting. Bruce saw that she was too tired to even pull her tail out after her.

There was no sign of Milton. Bruce's heart sank. His dearest friend was lost.

"Milton! Milton!" Angie cried, as she flew over the spot where she'd seen him last.

Carly's expression changed to one of pain and she groaned as she lifted her tail out of the ooze. With it came the most bedraggled spider Bruce had ever seen. Carly plopped Milton beyond the spot where they had fallen in and continued to crawl toward the clumps of grasses. Bruce hoped the footing was solid over there.

Milton didn't move. Bruce flew over and hovered above him. He touched Milton's face with his feet and brushed some of the ooze away, but the spider was lifeless. Milton's eyes stayed closed. He wasn't breathing.

"Milton!" Bruce cried. He landed on top of the spider and pulled the fur on his shoulders this way and that, hoping to wake him up.

Angie flew closer. "Reach into his mouth. Mud might be stopping him from breathing."

Bruce pushed more of the ooze away until he could see Milton's mouth. Opening it, he realized Angie was right. She landed near him and held Milton's mouth open while Bruce reached inside with his forefeet and scooped mud out.

"Angie—fly to the water and bring some back!"

She hurried to one of the nearby pools, drawing up the murky water just as she would nectar and then returned.

"Squirt it in his mouth to wash the rest of the mud away."

Angie shot the liquid into Milton's mouth, and Bruce did his best to remove the rest of the mud.

Milton still didn't move. He lay on his back with his legs curled.

Bruce knew this was how spiders looked when they died. His throat became tight, and he felt a heat rising inside. When he couldn't take it anymore, he cried, "Move back!" and he flew high into the air.

Turning over, he pointed his head to the ground,

folded his wings, and soared down. He crashed his shoulder into Milton's midsection. Bruce felt agony as his bruised and battered shoulder again exploded in pain. He stared at the spider and saw that more mud had pushed up and out of Milton's mouth. Bruce flew upward again, turned, and soared back down, crashing into Milton's stomach.

The spider coughed and convulsed and spit out a wad of mud. Bruce heard him take a quick breath, followed by more coughing.

Bruce fell to the ground and lay next to his friend with his eyes closed, the pain in his shoulder causing him to see streaks of light. When the ache subsided a little, he opened his eyes. Angie hovered above, and Carly was moving toward him.

Angie settled onto one of the mossy areas and fluttered her wings. As Bruce sat up, he could see that Milton still wasn't moving, but he *was* breathing.

"Carly—you saved Milton," Bruce said. "I can't—"

"Bruce, be quiet," Carly said. "How can anyone rest with you talking all the time?" She continued moving past and on toward a rivulet, where she let the water run over her body, cleansing away the mud. When she'd finished rinsing, she came back and lay on the ground next to him.

Bruce lay still, trying to block out the pain from his shoulder, trying to calm down. He'd almost lost his friends more than once before, but somehow this felt different. Perhaps it was watching them disappear before his eyes. Perhaps it was the fact that he'd led them into danger. Again. Maybe all of those things. He felt like crying, but he squeezed back the tears, concentrating instead on looking into the distance.

Out of the corner of his eye, he spotted something moving far to the left. He turned his head, wincing from the pain in his shoulder, and spotted a large spider headed their way. On the alert, he forced himself to stand up. "Come no closer, spider," he said, raising his wings. "We want no trouble."

Hearing these words, Angie turned, and Carly forced herself up from the ground.

The spider stopped for a moment but then advanced slowly, bouncing up and down, climbing over the moss. "I bring no trouble. I just want to know you."

Bruce realized from the voice that this spider was female. He felt more protective then, knowing she might attack Milton in his weakened condition, and he wouldn't be able to do anything about it. She was larger than Milton, but her shape was similar, although her coloring was different. Where Milton was brown, this spider had a black head and body, her legs were gray, and she had blue fur on her face and neck. Bruce thought she was both beautiful and terrifying.

He looked to Carly, his eyes pleading for help. She stood taller and faced the spider, clicking her claws.

"Go away," Carly said, moving forward to stand between the spiders. "Go away *now*."

The female spider stopped moving but stood her ground. "You will not be able to get across this bog without assistance. I could show you the way."

"Why do you want to help us?" Bruce asked, his tone harsh. He didn't trust this spider at all.

She swayed from side to side, and Bruce realized she also had that in common with Milton. He wondered if she was a jumping spider, too.

"I'd like to get to know *him*," she said, pointing at Milton. "If you're thinking I'll eat him—or *you*—don't worry. This bog offers treats in abundance, but I haven't seen another jumping spider in a long time. There aren't many of us in this part of the world." She moved closer, and Bruce saw that her back was patterned in silver. She really was quite beautiful.

"Our friend is recovering from being stuck under this moss," Bruce said. "Do you know how to help him?"

Angie scowled. "Why are you talking to her?" she whispered, moving closer to Bruce. "How do you know she won't just eat Milton, no matter what she says?"

"Because what she says makes sense. There's no end of food here for a spider. You've seen Milton grabbing flies and mosquitoes and crickets all along. I think she's interested in him because they're similar. I think Milton might also be interested in her."

"I am," Milton said, raising his head from the moss just a little. "But right now, I'm more interested in finding out why I can't stand up."

Chapter 14

Stung

"More than likely, you were stung when I lifted you out of that muck," Carly said. "The only way I could do it was to use my tail, and my stinger must have poked you. It should wear off soon. Well, if not soon, then eventually. I'm not sure how much venom you got."

Bruce looked up, trying to figure out how much daylight was left. He didn't want to be stuck here when it got dark. He didn't think they had far to go before reaching the river and Armand's home, but now they had to wait for Milton to recover …

It was as if Milton read his mind. "Why don't you leave me here and go on without me? I'll be fine."

"No. We're not going without you. End of subject." Bruce said, massaging his shoulder which still ached.

"Look, I wouldn't mind having some time to get to know this spider better, too," Milton said, and the new spider danced from side to side. "It will give me time to recover, and when you get back, I should be ready to travel. Right, Carly?"

Carly clicked her claws. "Probably," she said. "I don't know how much of my venom got into you, but since you can talk and move your legs a little now, it couldn't have been *that* much."

Bruce didn't think the female spider was going to eat Milton. Still, he didn't feel right about leaving Milton with her, or about leaving him at all. Perhaps the best thing would be for them to stay and go to Armand's some other time. Yet they'd come so far. He didn't want to have to go through this again, if he could help it.

He looked at the spiders. Milton still looked bedraggled, but he seemed to be rousing a bit. The other spider moved closer to him and began cleaning the mud and ooze from his fur.

"Milton, are you sure?" Bruce asked.

"Yes, Bruce. Go on. Go to Armand's, and when you get back, I should be fine."

"You're going to Armand's home?" the female spider asked.

"Yes," Bruce said. "Do you know him?"

"Of course. Everyone knows Armand. Why do you want to visit him?"

"We want to ask him some questions," Angie said, flying closer. "A friend of a friend has died, and we think Armand may know something about it."

Listening to Angie, Bruce realized it might not be a good idea to let everyone know why they were visiting Armand or the other suspects. This spider might be working for Armand.

The spider stopped cleaning and looked at Bruce. As if to confirm his thoughts, she said, "Be careful. Armand has spies, and he doesn't like others interfering in his affairs."

"Are you saying he's dangerous?" Angie asked.

"I've never known him to hurt anyone, but he knows what he wants, and he makes sure he gets it. Try not to get in his way." The spider stopped and said, "My name is Jemma. I'm pleased to meet you, but I don't understand how all of you can travel together."

Bruce sighed, thinking about Armand and spies and spiders that ate moths and salamanders that ate butterflies. There was always so much to worry about, he sometimes got tired from thinking about it all. "It's hard to explain. We made a pact to be friends and not eat one another." Seeing that Jemma still looked puzzled, he continued, "After we met, we realized it was more important to be friends and take care of each other than it was to follow our instincts." He looked at her closely and wondered if he was doing the right thing. "We'd like you to be a friend, too—especially a friend to Milton while we're gone." Having said that, Bruce realized he'd accepted Milton's suggestion to remain behind with Jemma.

"I'm glad you're making sense now," Milton said, waving a foreleg. "See, I'm better already. Go on. Oh, and be careful. I don't want to have to come looking for you. I expect to see you back here before sundown. Now get moving."

Jemma resumed her cleaning, and Milton *was* starting to look better. Bruce looked at Angie, who shrugged. "Carly, are you ready to go?" he asked.

"I've been ready to leave these lovers alone for a while."

Milton reddened and Bruce felt a pang of jealousy that surprised him. He lifted into the air and fluttered in the direction they'd been heading before.

"Just remember," Jemma called to them, "to avoid the light green moss. It isn't solid underneath, as you found out. If you stay away from that, you should be fine."

"Thanks, Jemma," Carly said, scooting to the right to put some distance between her and the green moss to her left. "We'll be back soon. Oh, and by the way—if you hurt my friend, I'll hunt you down, no matter where you go." She flicked her tail and walked away, following Angie and Bruce.

Jemma smiled and continued grooming Milton.

Chapter 15

Armand

Angie flew closer to Bruce. "Don't worry," she said. "Worry never helps. Besides, you wouldn't have left Milton there if you didn't think he'd be okay."

Bruce frowned, thinking about the spiders. He couldn't figure out what it was he didn't like about Jemma. She didn't seem threatening. In fact, as she was cleaning Milton, her movements were more like caresses, but something about her bothered him. "I don't know why, but I don't like her."

"Of course you don't. She's got the attention of your best friend," Carly said, as she picked her way through the muddy grass and weeds. "It's hard not to be jealous when someone you love begins to love someone else."

"I don't love Milton!" Bruce said, fuming. "Well, I mean, I *do* care for him, but I don't *love* him, not like *that.*"

"Great friendship is a kind of love," Carly continued, climbing over a large rock in her way. "You and Milton have been through a lot together. You're best friends." She stopped on top of the rock and looked up at Bruce, who circled overhead. "How could you not feel jealousy when someone new gets between the two of you?"

"I'm not jealous of Jemma. I don't even know her, and Milton doesn't love her."

Carly climbed down the rock. "Not yet."

Bruce flared and flew ahead a bit, trying to think straight. Carly had done it again. She had a way of latching onto his thoughts and feelings and throwing them out for everyone to see. For him to see. He knew she would do that when Agatha suggested bringing her along. He wished he hadn't listened. But even as these thoughts swirled in his head, he remembered how she'd helped save Angie when the frog swallowed her. And how she saved Milton from the muck, where he certainly would have died.

He thought about what she'd said about Milton. He *did* love Milton in a way. Not like he felt about Angie, but still he cared so much for Milton … it was hard to think about that and not feel it was something like love.

Whatever he felt about Milton and Jemma, Bruce decided it would be easier not to think about it right now and instead concentrate on where they were going. There were too many dangers around to allow himself to get lost in thought. Besides, all the thinking in the world wasn't going to change the situation.

He watched Carly scurrying along, trying to find the best route based on the path Bruce flew above. He could hear the sound of water flowing ahead of them. Suddenly Angie said, "There's the river!" and she flew ahead, leaving Bruce and Carly behind.

"Angie, don't go too far," Bruce said, peering ahead. They'd come to a downslope, and the river, sparkling in the afternoon sunlight, was in plain view.

"I just want to scout ahead and see where we're going."

"I'll be glad when we get out of this swamp," Carly said, shaking some dead, decaying leaves and ooze from one of her pincers. "This place smells bad."

Bruce said nothing. He really didn't want to start another conversation with Carly right now.

By the time Angie returned, they had gotten beyond the light green moss, and it appeared Carly was having an easier time since the surface was firmer. There were weeds and bushes and trees, and to their right was a pond surrounded by a grassy shore.

"The river is huge!" Angie said, landing on the stem of a nearby weed and spreading her wings wide. There's only one big rock in the entire area I can see, so I think we're almost there."

"Almost where?" came a thin voice from their right. Carly stopped, opened her pincers, and raised her stinger, ready to strike.

Angie flew backward, away from the direction of the voice.

Bruce joined her. "Who are you?" he said.

"I might ask you the same question."

"What do you want?"

"You are echoing my thoughts precisely. Please state your business."

"Show yourself first," Bruce said.

A crab scuttled out sideways from behind some weeds and faced Carly. His claws were open as well. Bruce was surprised that one of the crab's claws was much larger than the other, unlike Carly's, which were both the same size.

"As you wish," the crab said, waving his large claw in the air. "Now please tell me what you're doing here."

"I don't see why we should," Angie said, flying closer. "You don't own this swamp."

"No, but my employer does. Now state your business or go back the way you came."

Bruce decided this wasn't getting them anywhere, and if this crab did work for Armand, it would be easier just to talk with him. "We're here to visit Armand—your boss?"

"Yes. Do you have an appointment?"

"No. We want to ask him some questions."

"About what?"

"About none of your business," Angie said, flying closer still.

"Angie, get back. Let me do the talking," Bruce said.

Angie didn't budge. "Why should he have to know what we're doing here?"

"You're pretty spunky for a moth so small," the crab said, clicking his pincers at Angie.

Carly clicked hers more loudly in return. "You have no idea."

The crab scuttled sideways and back again. Finally he said, "Follow me. My name is Kyle. I will take you to Armand and ask if he will see you."

They followed the crab to the large rock that was partway on the riverbank and partway in the water. The river was wide and the current strong.

"Stay here," Kyle said, and he scurried into a hole beneath the rock and disappeared.

"I don't like him," Angie said. "He's bossy, and I don't see why he has to know what we're— "

"Armand will see you," Kyle said, reappearing from the hole.

Carly scuttled toward the crab, while Bruce and Angie flew close overhead.

"I'll go first," Carly said, "and make sure we have an agreement."

"An agreement?" said the crab, clicking his large pincer and tiptoeing in place.

"That we will not fight or try to eat one another during this visit."

Kyle smiled. "Of *course*," he said, his voice smooth. "That goes without saying."

"Well, I *am* saying it," Carly said as she disappeared into the burrow beneath the rock.

She was gone for only a short while. Bruce and Angie waited quietly, not speaking to each other or to Kyle. When Carly reappeared, she was followed by a medium-sized salamander.

Armand was brown with darker stripes. He walked with a limp and a cane, and Bruce saw that one of his back legs was scarred and twisted. Armand stopped when he was close enough to speak with the travelers.

"I am Armand. I understand you wish to ask me some questions. Please—come inside."

Bruce and Angie looked at Carly, who nodded. They flew down, landed not far from the scorpion, and walked toward the hole in the ground. Bruce noticed that Angie was trembling just a little, and he realized that he was also rather afraid of being underground with this salamander. Carly must feel it would be safe, and she would be there, but still ...

Bruce went first and walked through a corridor into a huge room with more than enough space to spread his wings and fly from one side to the other. He turned and saw Angie enter and look around, her eyes wide. Carly came next, followed by Armand. Kyle evidently remained above ground. Bruce wondered why Armand needed a bodyguard.

"Please—have a seat," Armand said, pointing to

a couch and several chairs that surrounded a low table. "May I get you something?" Armand moved to his cooking area, which was also quite large. It held many containers, and Armand lifted one, saying, "Some nectar, perhaps, or some pollen?" When no one answered, he placed that container down and reached into a cage, capturing a beetle that tried to fly away. "For you, my dear scorpion—may I offer you something more substantial?"

"Armand," Bruce said, ignoring the salamander's formalities, "we've come to ask if you know anything that might help us solve the mystery of Cecil's death. I assume you know he was murdered?"

Armand's expression grew somber. "Yes, I thought that might be it," he said, placing the beetle back into its cage. "I'm afraid I have nothing to tell you."

"Where were you on the morning of his death?" Angie asked, again surprising Bruce with her boldness.

"Let me see. Ah yes, I know. I was visiting one of my cousins who lives quite a distance from here. I had traveled there the morning before, and I was quite exhausted—you know, my bad leg and all." Armand came back from the cooking area and sat on a large cushion. "I stayed there overnight, and started back in the morning. I didn't get home until afternoon."

"Where does this cousin live? We'd like to visit and confirm your story."

Armand didn't seem to be offended, which surprised Bruce. "I can do better than explain. I'll draw you a map."

The salamander limped to his desk. It was made of a hard wood, and Bruce wondered how the salamander had come by it. Hard woods were difficult to cut and shape. Because of that, hard wood furniture was quite rare and costly.

Armand took out a sheet of paper, dipped a quill into an ink pot, and began to draw. When he finished, he brought the paper to Bruce. It was beautifully drawn and labeled in handsome script lettering.

"Vivian lives on the other side of the river. A bridge not far from here," he said, pointing to the map, "will bring you close to her home." Armand regarded Bruce. "I assume I am a suspect?"

Angie spoke before Bruce could answer. "We've been asked to investigate Cecil's murder, and we're treating everyone as suspects until we find out they didn't do it."

"Then you'll be talking with many, many creatures," Armand said. "I doubt all of the residents of the marsh will have an alibi—that is, something they can prove they were doing at the time of the murder." The salamander stretched his bad leg out straight. Bruce wondered if it caused him pain. "I believe you think me guilty because I wanted Cecil to leave the marsh and give up his land. That much is true—but I would not have killed him to get it. He and Elvira are the only residents still hanging on. The rest of the marsh, from this rock to the start of the forest, belongs to me."

"Why do you want own the entire marsh?" Angie asked.

"That, my dear moth, is my business," Armand said, sitting up again. He opened a small box on the table near him and withdrew a few small, circular globes, which Bruce recognized as eggs—quite like his own egg, in fact. Armand opened his mouth, popped the eggs inside, and swallowed. Bruce shuddered, thinking of the creatures who had just become Armand's snack. He decided they should ask the rest of their questions quickly and get out.

"Do you know who might have had a reason to kill Cecil?"

Armand reached for more eggs and held them in front of him, as he appeared to be lost in thought. "I would think Cecil's brother, Frederick, would have a motive—a reason—for murder. Both he and Cecil were in love with the same female. You should talk with Frederick when you visit Vivian, as they live quite close to one another. Vivian can tell you where to find him." He popped the eggs into his open mouth and smacked his lips after he'd swallowed them. "Ah, so very tasty. Would you like one?" Armand said, holding the box toward Bruce and Angie.

Bruce thought he might throw up, but he managed to contain himself. "Thank you for talking with us. If we have any other questions, we'll be back."

"Good luck in your search. Will you see yourselves out?"

Bruce walked toward the corridor outside, followed by Angie and Carly in the rear. When he emerged, the sunlight was fading. Kyle stood nearby and waved his claw, indicating they should follow him.

"We aren't going that way, at least not yet," Bruce said. "We need to find the bridge and cross the river."

Kyle pointed the other way and headed back to where he'd stood before.

"You're going there now?" Angie asked. "What about getting back to Milton?"

"I don't want to have to come this way again unless we absolutely have to," Bruce said. "Being this close, we should question Vivian and Frederick and get it over with."

"Do you think Armand did it? Do you think he killed Cecil?" Angie asked.

"I don't know. I did, before we got here. He *is* slimy, and I don't mean his skin. But if he really was visiting his cousin when Cecil was killed, he couldn't have done it. We need to check that out."

"You don't need to actually *do* the deed to be responsible for it," Carly said, flicking her tail. "Armand seems to have helpers who might have been here while he was conveniently away visiting a cousin. I don't trust him."

"I don't trust him, either, but I still want to talk with Frederick, and we'll check out Armand's alibi at the same time."

Chapter 16

Frederick

"Of course, I didn't kill him!" Frederick said, turning red from emotion and gesturing wildly with his forelegs. "He was my brother! I was angry, yes. Very angry. But I never would have killed him. I miss him very much."

Bruce wasn't used to seeing a walking stick who was alive, and he kept his distance from Frederick, who was very upset.

"Did you visit Cecil on the morning that he died?" Angie asked.

"No. I was there the day before, and we argued again. It pains me that the last words I spoke to him were spoken in anger."

"Where were you when the murder occurred?"

"I was here. If you're asking whether anyone saw me here, the answer is probably not."

"What was your argument with Cecil about?"

Frederick paced between his living and cooking

areas, still agitated. "I met Lydia at a party and fell for her. She is beautiful and charming, and my heart was hers from that moment. My brother was at that party, too, and he approached us when we were taking a stroll outside. I could see he was taken with her, and I became quite jealous. Cecil didn't care that I'd seen her first. He was like that: when he saw something he wanted, he took it. I steered Lydia away from him and asked if I could see her again. We courted for a while, until I discovered she was also seeing Cecil.

"I visited Cecil and told him to stop seeing Lydia, but it was no good. He said she loved him and, to prove it, he was going to ask her to marry him. I was furious.

"He asked her that same day, but she told him she couldn't make up her mind between us. That made *him* furious. He said, if she didn't know whether or not she loved him, he didn't want anything to do with her.

"When I found out, I was glad, thinking she would be mine, and we could be happy together. Then Lydia decided she loved Cecil best after all. She confessed her love for him, but he told her he wouldn't have her back.

"The day before Cecil died, I visited him and asked him to give her up to me. He said he already had. I was still angry that he'd intervened between Lydia and me, and we argued about other things, none of which matter now. I went home, and I was here the next day working outside. I don't have an alibi, although someone may have seen me in the garden."

Frederick paused. "You know, I'm glad Cecil did what he did. I realized the same thing he did: Lydia doesn't really love either of us. She's in love with herself."

"Would you tell us where we can find Lydia?" Angie asked.

"She lives north of here. I'll explain how to get there."

"Would you also happen to know a Vivian who lives nearby?"

"Of course. You wish to speak with her, too?"

"Yes. She may know something that will help with our investigation."

"She lives upriver also. Her home is in one of the burrows close to the river where the smooth stones are. By the way, Cecil's daughter, Polly, lives there, too." Frederick stopped his pacing and faced the travelers. "You know, I just thought of something else. While I visited last, Cecil told Horace he didn't want to talk with Orville, if he came by. It's possible that Orville could be a suspect."

"Who's Orville?" Bruce asked.

"He's a merchant, or at least that's what he calls himself. More like a trader. But some call him worse things. He preys upon those who don't know better or who are greedy. He gives them food or goods sometimes, and allows them to pay him back later.

When they do that, however, he demands they pay more than he gave them. And if they can't—I've heard it said that he will harm you or your loved ones. I steer clear of him. Cecil didn't, though. I don't know for sure, but I think Cecil may have owed Orville."

Bruce was busy making notes in his notebook. "Thanks for the tip, Frederick. We'll keep Orville in mind."

"I wish you luck. I hope you find out who did this to my brother."

"I hope so, too," Bruce said. He closed his notebook, and he and Angie and Carly moved on.

Chapter 17

The Warning

"I don't think we know a whole lot more for having come this far," Bruce said, as he and the others made their way back toward the bog. "Vivian said Armand was with her when Cecil was killed. Lydia's friend said Lydia was with her at the time of Cecil's murder. Lydia told us she wrote the note Milton found in the fireplace, so that clue is of no use anymore. Polly seems to have really cared for Cecil. We're left with a few more suspects to interview, but the ones I thought might have done it seem to be innocent."

"We need to dig deeper," Angie said.

Bruce flew down and landed ahead of Carly. "You've been really quiet. Not that I mind, of course," he said with a smile, "but I wonder what you're thinking."

The scorpion stopped and regarded Bruce. "If you had killed someone, and creatures you didn't know showed up and asked you questions about it, would you blurt out, 'Oh, yes, I did it, I killed Cecil'?" She continued walking, and Bruce lifted off the ground and flew above her. "No. You'd find a way to appear innocent. You'd get someone to lie for you.

"We know the killer planned a devious murder, hoping anyone asking about it later wouldn't guess how it was done. Then Agatha got involved, discovered the peanut oil, and knew Cecil would never have had it in his home.

"A killer devious enough to do that would be devious enough to cover his or her tracks. Maybe the killer hired someone else to do the dirty work. Then again, maybe Cecil's death really *was* an accident. Maybe Cecil used the peanut oil thinking it was something else.

"But, if Cecil *was* murdered, I'm thinking that if we stumble upon the killer and ask a lot of questions, we're opening ourselves up for harm, and we're not going to get any good answers anyway."

Bruce remembered why he didn't like talking with Carly. She always made sense, but it was never pleasant hearing it. "Do you have any better ideas?"

Before Carly could answer, a large shadow appeared over them. Carly scuttled under a nearby plant, and Bruce and Angie flew beneath the leaves of a tree, settling on one of the branches.

A large magpie flew down and landed on the ground where Bruce and Carly had been talking.

"Consider this a warning," the bird said, turning in a slow circle. "Stop this investigation, or you will be sorry." Then the bird flew away, and all was silent.

Carly was the first to come out. Seeing nothing, she motioned for the others to join her. "Guess we wore out our welcome."

Chapter 18

Milton and Jemma

They hurried back to the bog. Bruce kept thinking about the magpie and wondering who sent him. "Whoever sent the magpie has to be one of the suspects we talked with already."

"No," Carly said. "One of them could have told the killer we're here snooping around."

"She's right, Bruce," Angie said. "We're left more or less where we started, only now someone wants to hurt us if we continue. I think we should stop and let Agatha know what's happened so far."

"I don't want to tell Agatha we've found nothing."

"But the Magpie could come back and hurt or kill us," Angie said. "It's fine to try to find out what happened to Cecil, but if it gets us killed, no one is better off."

Bruce didn't deviate from the path he was flying. "Angie, other creatures try to kill and eat us every day. I don't want anything to happen to us, either, so we have to be careful. Listen—let's get back to Milton, make sure he's okay, and then we can talk more about it."

Bruce and Angie flew in silence and watched Carly pick her way over the vegetation and mud in the bog below. She was careful not to get close to the light-colored moss, and the way back seemed much easier than the first trip. Perhaps they were just more prepared for what was to come.

After they passed the boggy moss, Bruce started looking for Milton and Jemma. He was rewarded when he saw a large web with two spiders in it.

The larger spider, who had to be Jemma, waved a foreleg, and Milton did the same. Both spiders dropped from the web and performed a somersault in unison. "Welcome back," Milton said. "We were getting worried about you. We thought perhaps you liked Armand better than you like us."

Bruce settled onto a branch of a bush and Angie fluttered down next to him. She looked closely at Milton, who seemed ever so much better than when they'd left him behind. "How are you feeling?"

"I'm fine, now that Carly's attempt to kill me has worn off." Milton looked at the scorpion and smiled. "Remind me not to tangle with her in the future. There's no telling *what* she's going to do." He smiled again when Carly stuck her tongue out and made a rude noise. Turning back to Angie, Milton asked, "What happened on your trip?"

"We met with Armand. He was nice enough, but I still don't trust him. He said he was visiting his cousin, Vivian, when Cecil died, and he was too far away to be able to get back in time to kill Cecil. He suggested Frederick might be a suspect since he and Cecil had been arguing about a female friend. We—"

Bruce interrupted. "We visited Armand's cousin, Vivian, who said Armand was with her on the day Cecil died. Then we met Frederick, and, of course, he said he didn't kill Cecil, although he didn't have an alibi for the morning of the murder. He explained that he and Cecil both had a relationship with Lydia. It's kind of complicated. Lydia said she wrote the note Milton found in Cecil's fireplace, and a sample of her writing confirmed that. Lydia's friend said she was with her at the time of the murder. We visited Polly, and she said she was home at the time of the murder."

"Then we headed back this way," Angie said, before Bruce could say more, "and we were warned to stop investigating. A big magpie told us to stop asking questions, or else."

Milton's grin faded, and he swayed from side to side. "So, are we going to stop and go back to Agatha's?"

"We talked about that just before we got here," Angie said. "I felt like you do—that we should go talk to Agatha before we do any more snooping and someone gets hurt. Bruce doesn't want to go back and tell Agatha that we have no leads and lots more suspects. But Agatha said we should let her know if anything happened, so I think—"

"It isn't that I want to save face," Bruce said, a little red in the face nonetheless, "although I'd rather go back with something than nothing. What bothers me is that we must be getting close. Otherwise, whoever sent the magpie wouldn't be telling us to quit." He stretched to his full height and opened and closed his wings. "I don't like being bullied. It makes me want to keep searching even more than before." Bruce surveyed his friends. "Do you agree, or do you want to quit?"

Angie didn't answer right away. Milton was also quiet. Finally Carly spoke up. "For a change, I agree with Bruce. If we get scared away, someone gets away with murder. I think we should continue, but we have to be very careful."

Angie fluttered her wings and sighed. "I just don't want anything to happen to any of you—or myself, for that matter. If we die trying to find out who killed Cecil, that won't bring justice, and our families will be grieving for us, too."

Carly nodded. "That's so. But sometimes you have to take a stand for what you know is right, and it isn't right that Cecil's killer goes unpunished."

"I'll join your search," Jemma said, "if you'll have me along. Milton explained what you're doing, and I think it's a brave thing to do."

Bruce felt better about Jemma after hearing

this, even though he was still unsure of his feelings about her and Milton. He knew he should get to know her better before making judgments, but he was still upset that she'd moved into Milton's life so quickly.

Before Bruce could say more, Angie sighed and said, "All right. I'll stick with you, too."

Milton did a somersault, landed next to Bruce, and said, "Looks like we're still hunting then. Only one more thought: how about sending Horace back to Agatha, so she'll know to come as soon as she can?"

Angie nodded, and Bruce decided they were right. "Yes, we'll do that."

Milton tapped Bruce's notebook with his forefoot. "Who's next on our list to interview?"

"Cecil's students," Angie said. "We can see them on our way back to Horace's. The first one is named Nadine."

"Nadine it is, then," Milton said. "Who else after that?"

Bruce peeked into the notebook. "The only other students listed in Cecil's notebook are named George and Devon. We already know Devon found Cecil's body, so he's not a suspect. We should talk with George."

"We can't do all of that today," Angie said. "Not enough daylight left. We should probably camp here and go on in the morning."

Bruce nodded. "Right. So tomorrow morning,

we'll visit Nadine and George. After that, we'll see Horace and ask him to tell Agatha what's happened and what we're doing. Agreed?"

With nods all around, the plan was settled, and they started looking for a safe place to spend the night.

Chapter 19

Nadine and George

"Nadine was with me that morning," the mother shrew said, holding Nadine close to her side. Bruce had never seen shrews as small as these. "We were gathering twigs with her father so he could build a new work area."

Nadine was terrified. Bruce thought it must be difficult for such a small creature to believe that the spiders and scorpion wouldn't eat her.

"May we ask her some questions?" Angie asked her mother.

"Of course. Nadine—don't be afraid. These creatures won't hurt you."

Nadine didn't seem convinced, but she looked up at Angie.

"Did you see or hear anything strange the last time you took a lesson from Cecil?"

Nadine shook her head.

"Do you know anything that might help us find the creature who hurt him?"

She shook her head again, but a moment later, in a high, quavering voice, she said, "George's mama was angry. George visits Cecil after I do." She paused. "After I used to." A tear formed in her eye and she bowed her head.

"Do you know why she was angry?"

Nadine nodded. "Cecil said George's cooking wasn't very good, and he wouldn't let George enter the next competition."

"Do you remember what his mama said?"

"She said Cecil would be sorry."

Nadine sniffled, and her mother pulled her close. "Sounds like George's mother, Tanya, might be a suspect. They live down the path near the cattail glade. I hope you find out who did this. Cecil was a good teacher and very nice to Nadine. I'm sorry he's gone."

"We'll do our best," Angie said, as she flew back toward the path.

Bruce felt cheerful. "Maybe we'll find out George's mother did it and we'll be done searching. It would be nice to be done and be able to report back to Agatha that we did it."

"Yes, and then go home," Carly said. "I think I'm getting ready to molt."

"What's that?" Angie asked.

"That's when she sheds her body covering," Milton said. "It means she's growing. I do it, too."

"I never saw you molt," Bruce said, amazed he'd never heard of this until now.

"I molted not long after we'd gotten back from the first adventure and again after the last one. When you molt, you're very vulnerable. Your new shell is soft and easily damaged. I usually only molt when I can be alone for a while."

Bruce wondered if other creatures molted, too. He'd have to ask Grandpa Walter someday.

With the talk of molting, and going over clues and facts they'd gathered so far, the travels didn't seem as long. "Look—there's the cattail glade," Angie said, and she sped up a bit.

Bruce flew faster to catch up with her, and he saw not only a clearing ringed with cattails but also a gerbil. "That must be George, and look—he's brown with a white spot on his side that looks like a mushroom."

Bruce called the others to join him, and he spoke quietly. "If George is the gerbil who took Cecil's things, he may be the killer. We should be careful. We should surround him to be sure he doesn't run away, and you," he said, nodding toward Carly, "and you," pointing to the spiders, "shouldn't show yourselves right away. Angie and I will fly in alone first."

They continued getting closer. Carly usually moved quietly, but a twig cracked as she climbed over it, and George looked up, spotted Bruce and Angie, and waited while they flew closer.

"Are you George?" Bruce asked.

The gerbil frowned. "Who wants to know?"

"We just want to ask you some questions," Angie said.

Before they knew what was happening, the gerbil ran into the woods.

"We only want to talk with you," Angie said, flying after him.

The gerbil kept running until Carly reared up, blocking his path. Although he was larger than she was, her large claws and stinger tail must have looked menacing, and he stopped. Milton and Jemma appeared on each side, waving their forelegs and showing their fangs.

The gerbil glowered. "What do you want?"

Bruce took a different approach, knowing this gerbil was guilty of something. "We know you were at Cecil's home on the morning he was found dead, and we know you stole things from him. Why did you kill him?"

The gerbil trembled violently. "I didn't kill him! He was already dead!"

Angie spoke in a softer tone. "George, what did you take from Cecil?"

"It was nothing. Nothing special. I came for a lesson and found him—you know, just lying there. I decided he didn't need his stuff anymore—I mean, he was dead, and besides, I was mad that he wouldn't let me compete. He said I wasn't good enough."

Carly clicked her pincers. "What did you take?"

George's shoulders hunched over, and he seemed resigned to having been caught. "I'll get the stuff. Just keep *them* away from me." He walked back to the glade, and the others followed. He crawled into a hole next to the base of a tree. When he came out again, he was carrying a bundle and a larger gerbil followed him. George turned and said, "Mom, I told you it's okay."

"I'll see for myself," the mother gerbil said, scanning the group before her. "What do you want with my son?"

Bruce flitted closer and settled on the ground near the bundle. "We're investigating the death of Cecil. Your son stole some items from him. We came to get those and ask him some questions. We'd also like to know where you were that morning."

The mother gerbil bristled. "You think *I* killed him? You have some nerve. I didn't always like Cecil, and I was angry that he wouldn't let George enter this competition. But that doesn't mean I killed Cecil. I was here, and so was George. His father will tell you we were here." She stopped talking and looked at the bundle in George's paws. "Did you take those things?"

George looked down and scuffed his toes in the dirt. "Yes, but he was already dead. He'd never miss them."

"Give them back," his mother said. George dropped the bundle on the ground, pushing it closer to Bruce with his foot.

Bruce unwrapped the bundle. Inside were a book and some cooking tools. "We'll take these with us," he said, wrapping them again. "If we have more questions, we'll be back." Pointing at George, he said, "Don't run away next time."

Carly picked up the bundle and they continued on the path toward Horace's home. "I think they're telling the truth," she said. "When he saw Milton, Jemma, and me, George was too scared to lie anymore."

"I think so, too," Angie said.

"I still believe Armand did it," Bruce said. "I don't know why, but I think he's the one. Now all we have to do is prove it."

Chapter 20

Horace

As they continued through the marsh, the sky grew dark with clouds. The rain began as Horace's home came into view. By the time they reached it, lightning and thunder were frequent.

Bruce called out to the firefly. "Horace—may we come in? Horace?"

No answer. Bruce called again, but still no response. "Do you think he'd mind if we went inside to wait?"

"I think he'd think it would be silly of you to stand out here and get charred by lightning," Carly said, heading inside. The rest of them followed.

It was dark inside, and it took their eyes a moment to see well enough to move about. Bruce and Angie shook the water from their wings, fluttering to dry them. Bruce thought Milton and Jemma looked funny, with droplets of rain clinging to their furry bodies and legs. When a bolt of lightning struck close by, the room lit up, and

Bruce saw a bed, a table, household belongings, the normal things. The resulting boom of thunder made him think about crawling under the bed, like he did when he was a caterpillar.

Suddenly, Horace came flying in. He wheeled in the air, hovering above them. "Who's here? This is my home!"

"Horace, it's Bruce and the others—Agatha's friends."

Horace gazed at Bruce and settled on a bench close to his sleeping cot.

"I'm sorry we frightened you," Angie said. "It was raining so hard, we didn't think you'd mind."

"It's fine," Horace said. "I've just been somewhat unsettled ever since Cecil—well, you know. He shook his wings to remove the rain, creating another small shower of drops that wet everyone all over again. "Glad to see you. How did your research go? Did you find out who ... who ..."

Bruce shook his head. "Not yet. However, after the storm passes, we're hoping you might fly to Agatha's and give her the information we've collected so far."

"Of course. I must visit Armand and give him some information, too. I'll do that on my way back."

Bruce felt a prickle down his neck. "What kind of information are you taking to Armand?"

"About what the marsh creatures are doing. A new group of bees moved in near the edge of the marsh. I thought Armand would like to know."

"So Armand asks you for information?"

"He gives me good things to eat and drink, and shiny things. I like shiny things."

Bruce saw Horace had quite a collection of shiny items on shelves at the back of his room.

"Cecil used to do that when I brought information to him, too, before he ... died. When I told Armand about Cecil doing that, he started doing it, too."

Bruce was having trouble making sense of what the firefly was saying. "Horace—you say you brought information to Cecil. What kind of information?"

"In the beginning, Cecil wanted me to find out what happened in the marsh a long time ago. He was going to write it down so everyone could read it and remember. I liked doing that, because I got to know almost everyone. That's how I met Armand."

"You didn't know him before you visited to ask questions for Cecil's book?"

"No. He had only come to the marsh a little while before that, but he seemed happy to talk with me. He was really interested in Cecil's project."

The fur on Bruce's neck tingled even more. "Did you share Cecil's information with Armand?"

"Cecil had told me to say I was doing research for a book. He never said the information was secret. Did I do something wrong?" Horace seemed to be getting upset.

"No, Horace," Angie said, and she flew next to him. "You did just fine. Tell us what you told Armand."

Horace looked uncertain, but he continued. "Armand asked about my research, and I told him I did it for Cecil. Armand asked if I would work for him, too. I had to fly along those routes anyway while doing my research, so it seemed like a good idea to help him, too. Besides, he said he'd give me lots of shiny things."

Angie interrupted Bruce with a question. "Horace, let me ask you something different. You know George, Cecil's student, and his mother?"

"Oh yes. George has been Cecil's student for a long time."

"We understand Tanya and Cecil argued before he died. Do you know what the argument was about?"

Horace appeared to be unhappy. "Yes. Cecil's students needed his recommendation in order to participate in the local cooking competition. Cecil said George wasn't ready. That made his mother angry. She argued with Cecil, saying George was better than Cecil's other students. Cecil said he wouldn't change his mind." Horace buzzed his wings a bit. "I didn't like the arguing, so I started on an errand, but I heard Tanya say, 'You'll be sorry.' I'm not sure what she meant by that."

"That's probably enough questions for now," Bruce said, seeing Horace becoming agitated again. "We need to tell you what's happened to us so you can tell Agatha about it."

Horace brightened. "Please do!"

Bruce began the story of their research. Horace's eyes widened when Angie described being swallowed by the frog and Milton getting stuck in the moss and stung by Carly's tail. Milton explained about interviewing Armand, Frederick, Vivian, Nadine, and George, and told about the magpie and the warning.

Horace's eyes opened wide. "I can't believe all that's happened to you, and you still want to continue." The dragonfly stopped talking and cocked his head. "It sounds like the rain stopped. I'll leave for Agatha's right away."

"Please let her know we'll be waiting at Cecil's home. Oh, and Horace—don't tell anyone we came here today or that you're going to Agatha's, all right? The less anyone knows, the better. Especially Armand."

Horace nodded. "Absolutely. I won't say anything."

"We'll be on our way," Bruce said, heading outside. The rest followed.

"What do you think?" Bruce asked, after Horace had flown away.

They shook their heads. "No idea at all," Milton said. "Maybe Agatha will think of something we've missed."

"I hope so," Angie said. "But I agree with Bruce. I think Armand is the key to all of this."

Chapter 21

Angie

"Let's go over it one more time," Bruce said, pulling out his journal.

"Do you really think we'll come up with anything different this time?" Angie said.

"I don't know, but it's worth a try. We don't have anything better to do while we're waiting, do we?"

"Luxuriating in silence might be nice," Carly said. A tremor ran through her body, ending with a flick of her tail. "I definitely need to molt."

Angie gazed at Carly and said, "How can you tell?"

Carly shrugged. "It feels like my body is too large for my shell. Like I don't have enough room to breathe."

"Doesn't sound nice," Angie said.

"Actually, it is kind of nice," Jemma said, stepping forward to look at Carly's carapace. "When your shell cracks open, you suddenly feel free. You can move faster, and, as Carly said, you can breathe again. Maybe we should both molt."

"Didn't you say you're vulnerable and can't move around when you're molting? This might be a good time to do it, since we're stuck here, and all of us can protect you."

Carly surveyed the group with an odd expression.

"What's the matter?" Bruce said.

She scratched at the dirt floor. "I've never molted in front of anyone before."

Bruce found it difficult not to smile. "We won't look, then," he said. "I think Angie's right. This might be a good time to get it over with."

Carly thought about it and nodded. "All right—but just do whatever you were going to do, and don't bother about me. Okay?"

"Right. Jemma—are you going to molt, too?"

"It makes sense. Milton? What about you?"

"No, I molted not too long ago. I'm good for a while." He gazed at Jemma and said, "But I'll watch you, if you don't mind."

Jemma blushed and danced back and forth a little. "No, I don't mind," she said, smiling.

Bruce started to feel uncomfortable and motioned for Angie to follow him. "Want to go outdoors for a while? We can sit in the shade under the log and let these creatures do whatever it is they're going to do."

Angie nodded, and both of them flew outside.

They settled together on the ground beside the log not far from the opening.

"I never got the chance to ask how things have been going since I saw you last. What have you been up to?"

Angie glanced at Bruce and then looked away. "Not too much. Mostly the same old thing. It's been fun visiting with Carly recently. I didn't realize how much I missed her after our adventures were over, and we've had a good time."

Bruce nodded. "It's been that way with me, too, missing Milton. And you."

Angie nodded again. "I've missed you too, Bruce."

"You know you're always welcome to come and visit."

Angie looked at Bruce again and then gazed into the distance. "I know that. I've been pretty busy lately."

Bruce looked down, pouting a little. "You had time to visit Carly."

Both of them were quiet for a while. Finally Angie reached out with one forefoot and touched Bruce on the shoulder. "Bruce—I met a new friend. A moth friend. His name is Tom. We've been spending a lot of time together."

Bruce's heart sank as Angie's words took shape in his mind. At the end of their last adventure, he knew that he and Angie couldn't mate because she would become a moth and he would turn into a butterfly. But somehow he never thought about Angie finding someone else—loving someone else. His heart began to ache, and he suddenly felt very much alone. Before he could begin to sort out those feelings, an angry burning started inside his chest. He hadn't even met Tom, and already he disliked him. He stood and walked away from Angie, staring down the path. Looking away from her, he forced himself to say, "That's great, Angie."

"Bruce, you and I ... we share a special kind of love, and I'll always treasure it," Angie said, moving closer to where Bruce stood. "But I want more than just a wonderful friendship. I want to mate and have caterpillars of my own."

Her words floated in his mind, battling with the anger and hurt he felt. He imagined Angie with young caterpillars all around her. In his mind, he was still there with her. Suddenly, he turned to face Angie and held her forefeet in his. "We could adopt eggs or caterpillars, just like my parents did. Lots of eggs out there need good homes!"

Angie paused. "I thought of that, too, but then I met Tom, and things just fell into place with him. We're planning our mating ceremony. That's the real reason I went to visit Carly. I asked her to be part of our ceremony."

Bruce pulled his forefeet away and looked down the road again. "I see."

"No, you don't. I would have asked you next. I wasn't sure how I was going to tell you. This isn't easy for me, either, you know. I didn't want to hurt you." She paused. "Bruce, will you join in the ceremony with me?"

Bruce didn't have a chance to answer before he heard the sound of wings approaching. It wasn't a bird or a bat—the sound wasn't loud enough for that—but still he grabbed Angie and moved her closer, under the log and out of sight, in case it was a predator.

Amid a flutter of green wings, Agatha landed near them and dropped her satchel with a thump on the ground. After she touched down, she fanned her wings and folded them, all the while taking deep breaths.

"Agatha!" Angie cried, running out to meet the mantis.

"Angie, how wonderful you look! You are quite the beautiful moth, my dear! Hello, Bruce—didn't mean to frighten you. Is everyone all right? I came as quickly as I could."

"We didn't expect you to come, necessarily," Bruce said, feeling more powerless than before. He had hoped he would be able to solve the mystery and report back to Agatha that he knew who the killer was. Instead, they were no further ahead in the investigation, and he and the others had been threatened with harm if they continued. It was like he was a little caterpillar again, running home crying to Mom for help. "We just wanted you to know what was going on, in case—"

"In case something happened. Well, I'm not ready to face that outcome—not when it would be my fault." Agatha smoothed her wings again and exhaled a deep breath. "That trip used to be so easy, when I was younger. I'm showing signs of my age, huffing and puffing like this. Ah well, it can't be helped, I guess. Better advancing age than the alternative, I say." She scanned the area around them. "Where are the others?"

Bruce pointed to Cecil's home. "In there. Carly and Jemma are molting."

"Molting, eh? I had my last molt a long time ago, I think. Another sign of my age. Well, tell me more about what's happened to you. I have the bare facts from Horace—it was good that you sent him to get me. By the way, who's Jemma?"

"We'll explain everything," Bruce said. "There's a lot to tell."

Chapter 22

Pieces of the Puzzle

"I've read through the book we got from George," Bruce said, "and I still don't understand exactly what Cecil was doing with his research. Horace says Cecil was writing the history of the marsh. This book is definitely the start of that history, but it's pretty dull, if you ask me. All of these creatures and their offspring and their offspring's offspring, and who came from the outside, and what they did, and so on. Pretty boring."

"That's true," Agatha said, but I'm guessing there may be more clues there than we're aware of. Does he say anything about the local chefs, and, in particular, about Rodrigo?"

Bruce paged through the book. "Yes, here it is. 'Rodrigo was one of the great chefs of the marsh. He won many awards for his cooking, and he was often invited to oversee banquets for great dignitaries so he could prepare meals in their honor. He was very—'"

"I know about Rodrigo's cooking prowess," Agatha said. "Does it say anything about Rodrigo's death?"

Bruce scanned the rest of the page and turned to the next. "Maybe this is something. 'Rodrigo was known for his signature stew, made with sour yellow flowers he said were found only in this marsh. Many chefs tried to copy his recipe, but they were never able to reproduce his secret mix of ingredients. Some believe Rodrigo was gathering those yellow flowers when he drowned. His body was found lying in the shallow water of the bog surrounding the wetlands near the bridge. Numerous yellow flowers were floating in the water with him, but no plants having those flowers were found nearby.

"'Some thought his death was no accident, since Rodrigo had been a strong swimmer. However, no evidence of wrongdoing was ever found. Despite some who said he may have drowned himself, Rodrigo's death was eventually judged to be an accidental drowning.

"'During the investigation, suspects included several other chefs, any of whom might have wished to know the location of these flowers. However, the main suspect was—' Bruce stopped reading and looked up. "Agatha, it says here *you* were the main suspect in Rodrigo's murder."

Angie gasped, and the others stared at Agatha, who nodded.

"I knew you'd find out sooner or later. It's best to get it out now." She walked away, stretched her wings, and turned around to face them. "I used to live here in the marsh. Rodrigo and I were very much in love. He was dashing and handsome, and we spent most of our time together, either at his home in the marsh or mine. We were rivals with regard to cooking, of course, but we shared many ingredients and recipes, and the rivalry was friendly. All except when it came to his special yellow flowers. He let me taste one once. It was a bright yellow cup of a flower with five petals that grew high atop a long stalk. The stalk itself also had a pleasantly sour taste, and I enjoyed sucking the juice from it.

"One day late in summer, Rodrigo asked me to mate with him. I was so very happy—I'd longed for this, and we set a date near the fall harvest. After sharing the news with our friends and fellow chefs, we flew back to his home, where Rodrigo shared with me his source for the yellow flowers. It was his present to me as his mate-to-be. I was so honored, and I told him I would never divulge the secret to anyone else—a promise I was later forced to break."

Agatha paced. "I left his home late in the evening, carrying a bunch of the yellow flowers, which I placed into a closed basket for safekeeping at my home. The next day, I waited for him to come as promised, but he never did. Worried something had happened, I flew to Rodrigo's home, but he wasn't there. I searched nearby, but I didn't find him. Finally, I headed to the flower location he'd shared with me. He wasn't there either, but I noticed the mud near the edge of the water was covered with scratches—marks that looked to me as if a fight had occurred. I also noticed that quite a number of the yellow flower stalks had been recently cut, and a few were scattered on the ground.

"I was sure something terrible had happened. I flew back to the marsh and went to Cecil's, as I believed him to be the most able to investigate. Of course, I didn't think about the fact that I would be a suspect. When I wouldn't divulge the location of the flowers, Cecil said others would assume I had a part in Rodrigo's disappearance."

Agatha stopped pacing and stood with her eyes closed for a short while. No one said anything. Finally she continued. "His body was located the next day in the water near the bridge. I'm certain he was killed at the yellow flower spot and his body floated downstream until it settled there."

"What happened then?" Angie asked.

"Many of the marsh residents believed I killed him. They thought we'd mated already, and instead of eating him, as many mantises do, I drowned him instead." Agatha faced the travelers. "I can't see the need for doing away with my mate, although others seem to find pleasure in that … I'd prefer to have him alive." She sighed. "I miss Rodrigo even now.

"We searched for days to uncover more clues, but we never found out who did it. Cecil had no evidence linking me to Rodrigo's murder, which is what it was, and I was cleared of charges. Still, it was uncomfortable for me here after that, so I left the marsh, making my new home in the tree where I am now. This was one of the reasons I asked *you* to search for clues about Cecil's death—the marsh residents might not have thought as well of *my* asking, you see?"

Bruce was having trouble assimilating the information Agatha had shared in such a short time. Before he could ask anything more, Milton stepped out from Cecil's doorway and squinted his many eyes in the sunshine.

"Agatha! Good to see you," he said, bouncing up and down. He somersaulted and landed on her back. "Did you tell Agatha all that's happened?"

"Pretty much," Bruce said. "How's the molting coming along?"

"Jemma's done with her molt and Carly's not far behind."

As if on cue, a jumping spider appeared in Cecil's doorway. She was shiny, as if she had fluid all over her body. Bruce supposed it might be like his wings when he came out of his chrysalis. Jemma flexed her legs, pushed up and down several times, and walked toward Agatha, seemingly unafraid.

"You must be Agatha," she said, extending her forefoot in greeting. "Milton has told me many wonderful things about you."

"You have me at a disadvantage," Agatha said, touching her forefoot to Jemma's. "I had no idea Milton had a new friend."

As Milton walked back inside, Jemma said, "We met while Milton and the others were getting stuck in the bog. It was an awful experience, but one I'm glad for, too. If Carly and Milton hadn't gotten stuck there, I might never have met them and now you."

Just then, a great crash sounded from inside Cecil's home, followed by Milton's voice. "I'm all right. Everything's okay."

Agatha started toward the opening when Carly emerged, glistening with moisture. "What was the crash?" Agatha asked.

"Milton was helping me crawl out of my old shell, since there wasn't anything nearby to anchor it to. It came off all of a sudden, and he and the shell flew across the room."

Again, as if on cue, Milton walked out carrying what looked like a somewhat transparent copy of Carly. It seemed to weigh almost nothing. He danced around with it and finally set it down next to her.

Bruce thought it was strange to look at shells that looked so much like their owners but with nothing living inside. He thought it was creepy.

Milton carried the shell away, while Carly greeted Agatha.

"You'll need time before you're ready to travel," Agatha said.

Carly nodded. "Once our skins have hardened, we can go again."

"Bruce and Angie were about to tell me more about the book Cecil was writing and other things you discovered. Perhaps we can use the time while you harden to go over the facts again."

A fat raindrop hit Bruce on the head. He glanced up and saw dark clouds gathering again above the trees. "Looks like we'll be cooped up inside anyway," he said. "Another storm is coming."

Agatha gestured to the opening to Cecil's home. "After you," she said, and everyone went back inside.

Chapter 23

Trapped

Agatha's antennas waved back and forth as she recounted the facts. "Cecil thought he knew who killed Rodrigo, and it was a female, according to his note. She might also have killed Cecil, if she discovered that he knew what she'd done."

Angie spoke up. "If that's so, the female was someone who knew Cecil well enough to know he had an allergy to peanuts."

Agatha nodded. "You ruled out Lydia, who was with a friend at home and couldn't have done it. As far as we know, Polly had no reason to kill her father. The only other female suspect we have is George's mother, Tanya, but her mate said she was home at the time of the murder."

Bruce shook his head. "Of course, he could be lying. It's so hard to know what's true."

Agatha looked around the room. "Jemma—you haven't said anything. You must have some thoughts, too."

Jemma blushed. "I do, but ..."

"Don't be shy," Agatha said. "All ideas are welcome."

"It's not about Cecil's murder. I was thinking about the information Horace is bringing to Armand. I know why Cecil was gathering facts, but why is Armand so interested in what's going on? He's trying to own all the land in the marsh, and he's done that, or nearly so, with the exception of Elvira, who refuses to leave. Why does he want all the land? What's he going to do with it?"

Agatha nodded. "That does seem odd, and I don't have any answers. Since I consider Armand a prime suspect, I don't want to ask him directly what he's up to, although if he isn't doing anything wrong, he would probably give us the answer. I'll have to think about this some more."

Bruce was tired of thinking. In fact, he was simply tired and wondered when the others would decide to call it a night and go to sleep. He walked to the opening going outside and listened to the rain. The storm raged, and the water ran by like a small river outside the log, illuminated by occasional flashes of lightning. The rain was loud, and the sound drowned out what his friends were saying. Although wet, the weather wasn't particularly cold, yet he shivered.

He tried to spot Elvira across the path, but it was too gloomy to see much, especially a slug whose coloration matched the leaves. He saw movement from the corner of his eye. Was it a shadow he spotted farther up the path? When he turned to look, he saw nothing. He began to move back inside when he heard a noise behind him and, turning, he thought he saw something large move beyond the opening. He started to call out, but stopped, thinking himself silly for imagining things that weren't there. It must have been an owl or a shadow of some creature gliding by. He hadn't really seen anything, had he?

"What are you doing, Bruce?" Angie called from inside.

"Oh, nothing," he said. "Just watching the rain." But his senses told him there was more. He turned again, heading inside, when he heard a loud thud, and water splashed hard across his back and mud ran through his legs. The sound of the rain stopped.

Bruce whipped around and reached out. He felt a hard, wet surface where nothing had been moments before. It felt like a rock. He pushed. It didn't move.

"Agatha, come here!"

He heard a bustling and then Agatha was behind him, and the others were not far behind. Bruce stepped aside to let Agatha touch the stone. She pushed it, and it stood firm.

"Someone's trapped us in here!" Angie said, her voice shrill.

"Don't panic," Bruce said. "Stay calm. Let's try pushing together."

Bruce and Milton moved to one side, Jemma and Carly stood in the center, and Agatha moved on the other side with Angie.

"Now," Bruce said, and they pushed with all their strength. Nothing happened.

"Once more," he said, and they tried again, with the same result.

Agatha stepped back. "That's not going to work," she said, wiping mud from her forefeet. "We're not strong enough. We'll have to find another way."

"Perhaps we could carve away at the opening in the log," Angie said. "If we made it larger, we could crawl past the stone."

"That would take forever," Bruce said. When he saw Angie frown, he continued, "I mean, it's a good idea, but the tree's really hard, and none of us gnaw on wood."

"Bruce is right," Agatha said. "However, you've given me a different idea. The lightning that made this tree fall must have burned a hole in the side that is now the ground. If we work together, we might be able to tunnel underneath and get out that way."

"But we can't do that now," Milton said. "It's raining too hard. If we dig under now, the water will rush in and drown us."

"We could just stay here for a while. There's a lot to eat here," Jemma said. "I saw beans and seeds and pollen in Cecil's cooking area. I'm not hungry—I don't eat for a while after I molt. But

I know Milton can eat pollen. Agatha, you usually eat bugs, but can you eat other things? Is there enough here for the rest of you?"

Agatha looked grim. "I ate not long before I got here, so I don't need a meal for a while, but if we're stuck here for too long, all of us will be in trouble."

"We can't stay here," Angie said. "We have to find a way out! What if we run out of air? What if—"

"Angie, we'll find a way out. I know we will," Bruce said. Inwardly, he wondered how he would keep that promise.

Angie started walking around the room. The others seemed upset, too.

Suddenly, Carly walked to the fireplace. "Here's our way out."

Bruce laughed when he realized the fireplace had an opening that came out on top of the log.

"You're brilliant," Agatha said.

"I was just thinking," Carly said. "Even though it's bad that we're trapped in here, it's a good thing, too."

Everyone stared at her. Bruce thought she was probably really tired and didn't know what she was saying.

"No, really. At least this way, we know that no one can bother us tonight."

"Well, I don't think it's a good thing at all. My brothers trapped me in a hole once when I was a caterpillar, and now I hate being stuck in small spaces," Angie said.

Bruce sighed.

"I suggest we continue our discussion in the morning," Agatha said. Hopefully the rain will be done by then, and your shells will have hardened enough that we can travel. Meanwhile, it's been a long day. Let's get a good night's sleep. We'll get out of here in the morning, so don't worry. Especially you, Angie."

Chapter 24

More Pieces of the Puzzle

They decided to wait another day until both Carly and Jemma felt their shells were strong enough to climb up through the fireplace. Milton went first, and when he got to the top, he called that he'd made it out successfully. Bruce climbed next, and when he emerged, he laughed, pointing at Milton, who was covered with soot. Then he realized that he was probably just as black. He looked at his wings. All the beautiful colors were gone. He shook them and shivered his body, and a small cloud of soot settled around him, and also on Angie's head, as she emerged next from the chimney hole.

"Oh, that's awful!" she exclaimed, sneezing, and waving her antennas to clear her eyes of the black powder.

"At least you're out," Bruce said, helping her to move aside. "Next," he called down the hole, and Jemma's head appeared. She jumped next to Milton and brushed the soot from his back and legs. When she was done, Milton repeated the process with her.

Carly came next. Once she was out, she stood by the hole and waited until Agatha passed her satchel up through the opening. The hole was small in comparison to her size, but she squeezed and pushed, and Carly pulled, until she emerged, somewhat battered and completely covered in soot, but in one piece.

They climbed or flew to the ground where Bruce examined the large rock blocking the entrance to Cecil's home.

"Whoever put that rock there certainly doesn't want us snooping around," he said. "It's too large for anyone our size to move. It had to be a larger creature." He examined the area around the rock. "I don't find anything that might show who did it. The rain washed any footprints away." Bruce shivered, again realizing the seriousness of what they were doing. "Someone actually tried to kill us."

"I can't be sure," came Elvira's voice from across the path, "but I think I saw a rat out there last night."

"A rat would be large enough to move that stone," Angie said. "Are there rats living here in the marsh?"

"Of course," Elvira said. "Rats are everywhere. Not like the rest of us, who need certain types of plants or conditions in order to survive well. I'd never be able to live in a desert in the hot sun, for example—I'd dry up and blow away! But a rat—a rat can live anywhere."

"Where do they live around the marsh?" Milton asked.

"Most of them are on the other side of the river now. Armand made some kind of deal with them a long time ago. The rats moved away, and that was the start of Armand owning this side of the marsh."

"Maybe we need to make a visit to someone across the river and find out what the rats are up to," Angie said. "Perhaps we can get more information if we ask other creatures we've already met to help us. I'm thinking of George and his mother, for example. They might be able to talk to the rats without arousing suspicion."

"Before I go anywhere, I'm getting the rest of this soot off of me," Bruce said, as he flew over to one of the pools remaining from the rainstorm. Every wingbeat left a small puff of black powder wafting in the air. The others followed him, and while some of the soot was hard to remove, most of it came off in the water, which was now quite black.

Agatha sat by the side of the road and spoke to the others as they finished their cleaning. "Our search for Cecil's murderer has definitely put us in danger. Bruce is right. Someone tried to kill us last night by sealing us up in Cecil's home. I'm no longer comfortable with you being here. I want all of you to go home."

Bruce shook the last of the water from his wings, purposely showering the drops onto Milton and Jemma, who hunched their shoulders and made faces at him. "I know you want to keep us safe, and I appreciate that, but I'm not going. I'm old enough to choose for myself, and I won't let a bunch of thugs scare me away." Bruce looked at Agatha and his gaze never wavered. "I won't be bullied anymore. Cecil was murdered, and his killer shouldn't get away without punishment."

The travelers murmured agreement and Milton stepped forward. "I don't want to see anything happen to us, but we need to stay together and discover the truth."

The rest of the party nodded.

Jemma raised her foreleg. "There's something I don't understand. If we do find out who killed Cecil, what then? How would he or she be punished?"

Agatha tilted her head. "Good question, Jemma. Usually, the best that can be done is to send such creatures away. They become as good as dead to those who knew them. Often they are branded—given a mark—so that other creatures who meet them later know they did wrong, so they are not welcome. It's a sad, lonely existence. It's the best justice we can make."

The rain started again, and once more they sought shelter at Horace's home. Horace wasn't there. The room was the same, except for a large, open container of small round globes.

Bruce walked toward the container and took a closer look.

"What are they?" Milton asked.

"They look like eggs," Bruce replied. "They could be butterfly eggs."

"Or moth eggs," Angie said.

"Lots of eggs look like that," Jemma said, coming closer to get a look. "The question is, why are they here?"

Agatha noticed a note on Horace's table. She read it and motioned for Bruce to come closer. "Look."

Bruce read it aloud. "'Bring eggs to the bridge.' So Horace is delivering eggs to someone."

"Not just *someone.* Look at the writing. See the way the letters are formed? Don't they look familiar?"

Bruce studied the note again, and his eyes widened. "This is from Armand! The script is the same as the map he gave us. So Horace is delivering these eggs for Armand. I wonder where he's taking them?"

They heard a buzzing outside, and a voice called, "Agatha?"

"Yes, Horace. We came in again to get out of the rain."

Horace flew inside and settled on his bed. He shook his wings, sending another shower of droplets onto everyone.

"You're quite welcome," Horace said. "Actually, the storm seems to be passing now." The dragonfly walked toward the container of eggs. "I overheard what you said. I'm not delivering the eggs *for* Armand—I'm delivering them *to* Armand. This note was with the eggs when I picked them up."

Carly lifted one of the eggs and looked at it. "So Armand asked you to bring these? Who gave them to you?"

"I picked them up at the bridge, but I don't know who left them there. I pick things up for Armand all the time. I used to think Orville was bringing the stuff, but he said he didn't know anything about it."

Agatha seemed confused. "Who's Orville?"

Horace smiled. "Everyone knows Orville. He's comes here to trade things. He brings lots of nice, shiny things. Cecil used to give him food in exchange for cooking ingredients."

"But you say Orville doesn't bring these 'gifts'?"

"No. I saw Orville when I flew to the other side of the river to pick up some seeds at the bridge. He said he had no idea where the gifts come from."

Bruce cocked his head, trying to figure out who would be sending "gifts" to Armand. "Do you always get these 'gifts' at the bridge?"

"No. All over. Armand tells me where to pick them up, and the gifts are always waiting when I get there. Last time, I had to go to the fork in the river where the cattails start and get a basket of feathers.

Sometimes it's eggs, like this, or seeds or nuts or spices or fruit. All I know is that I'm supposed to pick things up and bring them back to a spot where Armand sends someone else to pick them up. I brought these eggs home this time because it was raining so hard, and I didn't want them to float away. I have to deliver them when the rain stops."

Agatha raised her forefeet, signaling to the others to stop asking questions. "Horace, thank you. That's enough for now. Oh, and thank you again for letting us shelter here. I believe the rain *has* stopped, and we can be on our way."

Everyone filed out, and when Bruce looked up, he saw a rainbow. He glanced toward Angie and started to point it out to her, but she was flying low, talking with Jemma and Carly. Bruce frowned, realizing she hadn't sought his company very much during this trip. *Now that she has a moth friend,* he thought, *she doesn't need a butterfly friend anymore.*

Agatha pointed to a shallow ledge just off the path and headed toward it. When all the creatures had gathered, she said, "We seem to be finding more questions than answers. It's time to decide what we're going to do from here."

"I may have an answer," Jemma said, and everyone turned. "I was thinking about Armand and the eggs at Horace's home. The note you said was in Armand's writing came with the eggs Horace picked up. That means Armand sent the note to someone else who brought the eggs to the bridge. I don't think they're really 'gifts' at all. I think they're payments."

Angie's antennas wiggled, and she squinted her eyes. "Why would other creatures pay Armand? What does he do for them?"

Jemma shook her head and shrugged. "I don't think he's doing anything. I think they're paying him *not* to do something."

"What do you mean?" Bruce asked, more confused than before.

"I don't know for sure, but Horace said Armand is having him gather information, just like Cecil did. Maybe Armand learned things about the other creatures in the marsh, just like Cecil did—things they don't want anyone to know. Maybe they're paying Armand to keep quiet."

Agatha tipped her head sideways, and her eyes sparkled. "Jemma, you may be right. It's even possible that Armand also discovered who killed Rodrigo and is demanding payment from the killer to keep silent."

"So we need to talk to the rats and also Orville," Bruce said. "Both of them are on the other side of the river. I hope we can find another way there without going through the gooey marsh and by Armand's place. Maybe Elvira would know—wait!" Bruce pointed up and the others saw Horace flying toward them, carrying the basket of eggs. "Horace will know if there's another way there. Horace!" Bruce motioned to the dragonfly to come down.

"I can't stay," Horace said, as he hovered in the air above them. "I'm late now as it is."

"Can you tell us a different way to get to the river and the bridge without going through the gooey marsh and by Armand's home?"

"Travel north until you reach the big, black road. Follow that to the river. Be careful—the human machines travel there, and it's quite dangerous."

"Thank you, Horace. May your travels be safe."

The dragonfly zoomed away, and the friends headed north.

"I'm glad we don't have to go through that marshy ooze again," Milton said. "If I never see a bog again, it will be too soon."

"Even when it comes with beautiful, female spiders?" Jemma asked, trying to appear hurt.

Milton blushed. "Well, maybe bogs aren't quite as bad as all that," he said, and he began running as Jemma chased him up a tree.

Chapter 25

Sam

Following the road on the way to the bridge was much faster than their trip through the marsh had been, and the rain hadn't returned, although gray clouds still covered a good portion of the sky. Several times they had seen large machines that men used on the road. They were careful to stay far away from those, under the bushes and in the trees, to be safe. The machines were loud, and they smelled terrible. Some of them belched gray and black smoke. All of them crushed the weeds and creatures who were unlucky enough to be in the road when they rolled by.

The bridge was much larger than Bruce had thought it would be—wide enough for the machines to cross. It rose high in the air over the center of the river and back down on the other side. The group crossed it easily, but as Bruce flew over it, he couldn't help looking at the river which now ran very fast due to the added water from the rains.

As they traveled along, they asked everyone they encountered if they'd seen Orville, the trader. Two small skinks by the side of the road hadn't seen him, nor had the wasps, crickets, or the beetles who were busy rolling their small balls of dung. Bruce was beginning to think this trip might be fruitless when Agatha said, "Bruce, look. There's a butterfly up ahead near the trees. Why don't you go ask if she's seen Orville."

Bruce gazed in the direction Agatha pointed. He spotted the butterfly, and his wings stopped beating. He had to flutter quickly to avoid dropping to the ground. Finally pumping his wings, Bruce flew higher and landed on a bush where he tried to compose himself.

She was the most beautiful butterfly he had ever seen. Her wings were rounded and had small crescents of orange and yellow around the edges. Beautiful brown fur covered her body and her antennas were special, too: furry and black, with thin white stripes to the tip, which was brown like her body.

Bruce faced his friends and said, "Angie, why don't *you* talk with her?"

Angie shook her head and smiled. "No, I'm sure she'd rather talk with *you*, Bruce. Go on."

He could tell from the smirks on their faces that they wouldn't go anywhere until he'd talked with her. Sighing, Bruce lifted off the bush and headed her way. His stomach knotted, and his heart beat much too fast. When he got closer, she spotted him and circled in the air. She landed in a tree, and waited for him to come near.

"Hello," he said, fluttering back and forth. "We're looking for Orville, the trader. Do you know where he might be?"

The butterfly smiled, and Bruce's heart did a little flip-flop. "Yes, I do," she said, and her voice was smooth, like warm nectar. "He was here just a little while ago, and he went that way," she said, pointing up the road in the direction they'd been going. "If you stay near the road, you should find him soon." She gazed at Bruce, and he saw that her eyes were beautiful, too, with their many facets shining like sunlight on water. "I haven't seen you before."

Bruce tried to answer, but his voice cracked, and he had to swallow first. "We don't live here," he said, fluttering by her again. "We're investigating a murder."

Her eyes grew wide and she drew in a small breath. "A murder? Who was killed?"

"Did you know Cecil, the chef? He lived in the marsh on the other side of the bridge. He died a few days ago."

She shook her head. "No, I'm not from around here, either. I only came to visit my sister. I planned to go home today, but she said the trees here had some nice nectar in their flowers, so I decided I'd sample them first. She was right. You should try some before you go on."

Bruce looked around and saw that the rest of his group had settled down for a rest, so he figured it might be all right if he joined her for a while. He landed on a flower nearby where she stood and extended his forefeet toward her. "My name is Bruce."

She raised her forefeet and touched his. "Pleased to meet you. My name is Samantha, but everyone calls me Sam."

Bruce smiled. "I like that name," he said, thinking his reply sounded really dumb, but it was all he could think of. He unrolled his tongue into the flower and sucked the nectar from inside. He loved the tangy sweetness. "Mmm, that's good. Thanks for telling me about these."

Sam fluttered around Bruce and landed on the other side of the flower. "How will you find the creature who killed your friend?

"We hope Orville might have information that will help us."

"Your friends—those are your friends?—you don't eat each other?"

"Yes, they *are* my friends, and no, we have an agreement. We're like family. Come—I'll introduce you."

They flew toward the others, and Bruce made the introductions. As Angie said hello, Bruce thought she appeared upset. He wondered if Angie felt the same way he had earlier, when she told him about her new friend, Tom.

"We should be on our way, Bruce," Agatha said. "I want to find Orville before he decides to go a different way and we lose him."

Bruce looked stricken. He had never met a butterfly like Sam before, and he didn't want to say goodbye. He didn't want to lose her before he'd had a chance to get to know her. "Sam—do you live around here?"

She shook her head. "No. I live north and west of here, across the river near the forest. I was heading there, after I had my fill of this nectar. Would you mind if I go with you, at least until you find Orville?"

Bruce couldn't believe what he was hearing. She wanted to go with them. With *him*. "Yes, I mean, no—I mean, of course, we would like that." Bruce felt the color rising in his face, and the knot in his stomach grew larger. "That would be great," he said, looking around at the others who nodded—all except Angie, who still had a look he couldn't decipher.

"Let's go, then," Agatha said, and she opened her wings and headed up the road.

Chapter 26

Orville

When they spotted Orville, they knew him immediately, despite having had no description of him ahead of time. He was a medium-sized woodchuck, although it was difficult to tell what color he was because he was covered with various kinds of baskets, containers, tools, and bits of junk. He rattled when he walked, as the things he carried shifted left and right as he waddled along.

Agatha motioned for the group to stop and gather close to her. "Let me do the talking, please. I don't know if Orville is as devious as Frederick led you to believe, but, just in case, I'd rather treat him cautiously."

Everyone nodded, and Agatha flew close behind him, calling out a greeting. "Hello—would you be Orville?"

The woodchuck stopped and waddled in a circle until he was facing her. "The very one!" He tried to bow but found himself unable to do so because of everything he carried. "May I be of service?"

The rest of the party caught up to Agatha and looked at this creature, who looked more like a walking collection of junk than a woodchuck.

"We are investigating a murder," Agatha said, at which the woodchuck backed up slightly and raised his forelegs off the ground. His containers and implements clanked and rattled, and his eyes opened wide. "Did you know Cecil, the chef, who lived across the river?"

"Oh, my, yes! I was so sorry to hear about his death. But murder! Who would murder Cecil?"

"Who, indeed?" Agatha said. "We're hoping you may have information that will help us locate his killer."

"I don't know anything about that at all," Orville said, lowering his body down again. "I was in that area a few days ago, and I planned to visit Cecil and see if he needed any new cooking tools. I'd gotten quite a bargain on some long spoons I thought he'd like. But Horace, the dragonfly who works for him, told me Cecil didn't want to be disturbed, so I continued on my rounds. Alas, I won't be visiting him now, will I?"

Bruce thought the woodchuck seemed genuinely unhappy.

"In any case," Orville continued, "I haven't actually seen Cecil for a moon's time or more."

"When you talked with Horace, did you notice

anything out of the ordinary?"

Orville considered this and shook his head. "No, nothing—although it was a little odd that Cecil didn't want to at least say hello. We've always enjoyed our conversations, and he liked getting the news from my travels through the marsh."

"I have some questions about other residents of the marsh, if you'd be so kind. Since we're looking for a murderer, it's difficult to question the residents, because most likely the killer is one of them."

"Oh, yes. I see." Orville settled back on his haunches and put his paws together. "Well, you know, I make my living trading in items of value, and I'd say my information might have value to you. Would you agree to a trade? Something of yours for something of mine?"

Agatha's eyes became a bit more beady, but she opened her satchel and pulled out something covered in a bit of cloth. She unwrapped it and held the contents toward the woodchuck, who leaned forward to smell it, his containers rattling as he moved.

"Ooh, apple cakes!" he said, and his nose twitched as he inhaled the delicious smell. "Yes, those will do nicely. What would you like to know?" He reached for the cakes, but Agatha pulled them back.

"Before we begin, I want your promise that you will not tell anyone about the questions I'm asking today. Do you agree?"

"Yes, of course."

Agatha held the cakes out again, and Orville was quick to take them this time.

"All right. First, please tell us about Armand."

"Hmm. Armand is a difficult creature to explain, and I am not sure I know about everything that Armand does."

"Do you think it's possible Armand is blackmailing other creatures here in the marsh?"

Orville looked surprised. "He has a bad reputation, that's true, but as for blackmail—I couldn't say."

"What is blackmail?" Angie asked.

"Blackmail, my dear, is when I know a secret about you and I threaten to tell it unless you pay me to keep quiet. It's quite common, really."

Bruce glanced at Jemma and nodded his head, confirming she had been right with her earlier assumptions.

"That's terrible! Why would someone do that?" Angie said.

"Yes. Blackmailing someone is wrong—but, in order to be blackmailed, you must also have done something wrong, too. In a way, you could consider blackmail as a proper punishment, couldn't you?" Orville scratched his chin and continued. "Beyond the blackmail, I know Armand wants to own the land in the marsh and, once he has it all, he plans to build a canal. Why? I don't know, but Armand said it will make the marsh a better place."

"But if all the residents of the marsh have to *leave*

the marsh," Bruce said, "how does that help them?"

Orville shook his head. "I don't have those answers, nor do I know Armand's thoughts. I do have sources who tell me things, and I'm sharing what I know with you." He paused and popped the apple cakes into his mouth. His expression changed to one of bliss, as he chewed and swallowed the small morsels. "My compliments to the chef," he said, gathering up the crumbs and inclining his head toward Agatha. "Those were excellent."

"So you don't think Armand murdered Cecil to get his land?" Bruce asked.

Orville's whiskers twitched. "I wouldn't think so. Do you have other suspects?"

Agatha nodded. "Too many. Bruce—read your list."

Bruce opened his notebook and read aloud. "Lydia, who was the girlfriend of both Cecil and his brother, Frederick, until both of them stopped seeing her. Then there's Frederick himself, and also Cecil's daughter, Polly, both of whom would inherit whatever goods Cecil had. George, one of Cecil's students, and his mother were upset that Cecil wouldn't let George enter an upcoming cooking competition. We are also wondering if Cecil's murderer might be the same creature who killed Chef Rodrigo. One of the notes Cecil left behind indicated he'd learned who murdered Rodrigo and that the creature was female. That points to Lydia, Polly, or George's mother as the best suspects."

"You're forgetting Isabelle," Orville said. "Since she was one of the major suspects, after yourself, of course, in Rodrigo's death, I'd be sure to include her on your list."

Agatha looked flustered, and she reddened.

"Of course I know who you are," Orville said. "I also know you were cleared of any wrongdoing. Perhaps because of your being suspected of Rodrigo's murder yourself, you didn't know Isabelle was also questioned?"

Agatha shook her head. "Truly, I didn't. But she must have proven her innocence?"

Orville sat down, wincing, and his pans and implements clanked and creaked. "I'm getting old, and my joints ache. They make almost as much noise as this other stuff," he said, smiling. He looked at Agatha's satchel. "Would you have any more of those delicious cakes?"

"I do."

Orville's face brightened as Agatha reached into her satchel and produced four more cakes, which she passed to the trader. "What can you tell us about the suspects we mentioned?"

"Mmph, yeph," Orville said, his mouth full of cake. When he'd swallowed, he appeared much happier. "Lydia is flighty and emotional, but I don't think she would kill just because she was jilted. On the other hand, love can turn to hate, and it can be a powerful motivator. Still, it's not in her nature, and, the last time I saw her, she was still crying over Cecil's death. I don't think that would be true if she'd done him in. Who's next on your list?"

"Polly."

"Cecil told me Polly was a good daughter. She came by often to talk with him. I don't think she had any reason to kill him—certainly not for an inheritance. Most of the things Cecil owned aren't worth much to anyone who doesn't love cooking, and Cecil once told me that Polly can't even boil water. Besides, Polly is well off on her own, so I think you could scratch her from your list."

"How about George's mother?"

Ah. Tanya—that's her name—has a temper. She's overly protective of her spoiled brat of a son, and I think, given the right moment, she or George might have lost their temper enough to kill. I don't like to speak ill of my clients, but Tanya and her son have done me wrong a time or two in the past. They're not my favorite creatures. Leave them both on your list."

"You mentioned someone named Isabelle. Who is she?" Bruce asked.

Orville looked at Agatha. Her expression appeared somewhat sad and serious, but she inclined her head and nodded slightly, indicating he should proceed. "Isabelle—" Orville paused, as if trying to figure out how to say what was in his mind. "It's quite possible Isabelle had something to do with this. She hasn't been quite right, ever since Rodrigo died. Agatha—you were too busy answering questions to have seen all that went on with Isabelle at that time." Orville waved one of his paws at the rest of the group. "Do they know about Rodrigo and everything that happened?"

Agatha nodded. "They know about Rodrigo, and about my having been a suspect in his murder. I didn't tell them anything about Isabelle."

"No one believed Rodrigo drowned by accident because he was a great swimmer. When you were cleared as a suspect, attention shifted to Isabelle, who'd also had a relationship with Rodrigo at one time. However, Isabelle swore she was with her brother at the time Rodrigo died. She and Armand have always been very close—she even went to live with him for a while after the murder."

Agatha appeared flustered. "I never knew Isabelle and Rodrigo had been together."

"Wait," Bruce said, closing his notebook. "Isabelle is Armand's sister?"

"Yes. She has always been devoted to Armand, and he to her. When they are together, it is hard to tell them apart, they look so much alike, except for Armand's bad leg. Anyway, I know Isabelle visited Cecil from time to time. What their dealings were, I'm not sure, although I know that Isabelle, being another chef, was in competition with Cecil. Perhaps she was upset about Cecil's decision to rejoin the cooking competition, after being away from it for so long. It would've been harder for her to win with Cecil there."

Bruce reopened his notebook and made notes. When he finished, he looked back at a previous entry and said, "Cecil's note to the Commissioner makes sense if Isabelle is the killer. Remember, his last sentence says, 'I will continue to look into it as I can, but the chef I' and a squiggle. Maybe the 'I' wasn't meaning Cecil. Maybe it was the beginning of the name 'Isabelle.' If Cecil thought Isabelle killed Rodrigo, maybe she found out and killed him to stop him from saying anything."

Orville nodded. "That could be. Now you asked about some other suspects also. I'm happy to answer more questions, if you have more of those wonderful cakes."

Agatha reopened her satchel and looked inside. I don't have any more apple cakes," she said, and Orville frowned a little, "but I do have a plum tart."

At the site of the tart, Orville's eyes grew large. "Oh, yes, please."

Agatha passed the tart to Orville, who swallowed it whole. "Mmm, very tasty. You are a marvelous chef."

"Of course I am," Agatha said. "Now—tell us about Frederick."

"He had a reason for murder, as I said before—a reason named Lydia. Frederick was very angry with Cecil. I heard that Frederick thought Cecil stole Lydia from him. You see, Lydia was dating both Cecil and Frederick. When Cecil asked her to mate with him, she couldn't decide which one she loved more. Cecil became angry, and he said he didn't want to see her anymore. That made her realize she loved him most, but it was too late—he'd given her up. Then Frederick told Lydia he didn't want her either, so Lydia was in a mess. Do I think Frederick would kill Cecil? Perhaps, in a fit of rage … yet, I think some of your other suspects are better candidates. Truly, I think the best suspect would be—"

Chapter 27

Attack

The attack came without warning. Before anyone realized what was happening, rocks crashed around them. Orville fell over and lay still. Everyone else ducked and ran.

"Get under cover!" Agatha shouted, as she ran behind a tree. Milton and Jemma bounded after her. Bruce, Angie, Carly, and Sam went the other direction across the path. When they made it to the other side, they were suddenly swept off the ground and into the air, caught in a net of fibers. They spilled down on top of one another as the net rose higher and higher into the air. Great pains shot through Bruce's wings, and he realized that he and his friends had been caught in a trap.

"Help! Agatha! Milton!" was all Bruce could say before the net dropped, dashing the four of them on the ground. Bruce felt more sharp pains in his wings as he collided with Carly's back. It took him a moment to realize the net was being dragged along the ground, through the underbrush and into the trees.

"Agatha! Milton!" he called again, but whoever was dragging them moved very quickly, and he didn't think any of his friends would be able to catch them.

They were dashed against sharp rocks and sticks as they tumbled along. The pain in Bruce's wings grew worse, and he realized the net was rising again, this time onto the back of the creature who'd dragged them away.

He managed to get a breath and tried to force the pain aside. "Are all of you okay?" he asked, his voice shaking.

"I'm bruised, but it's not serious," Angie said.

"I'm okay," Sam said. "My wings hurt a little at first, but I think they'll be fine. Where are we going?"

"If I could turn over, I might be able to sting this creature," Carly said, struggling within the net. Her legs kept going through the holes, and she was only becoming more tangled.

Bruce looked at his wings and felt a stab of anguish. The larger one on the right side had a long gash near the top, and the smaller one was bent and broken. He wondered if he would ever fly again.

"Where are you taking us? Who are you working for?" Bruce called. "We have resources and can pay if you let us go."

The creature turned his head around as he continued bounding through the trees. Bruce saw that he was furry and brown and looked a lot like Lilly. His face seemed so familiar ... Bruce couldn't believe it could be the same weasel, but he looked like Lilly's brother, the weasel they'd met so long ago on the boat going to the island. *What was his name? Think! Edward? No—let's see. Oh, yes!*

"Eugene?"

The weasel stopped and dropped the bag, and the creatures inside tumbled on top of one another. Bruce winced again, but he looked up at the weasel, sure now that this was Lilly's brother.

"How do you know my name?"

"You don't recognize me because I'm no longer a caterpillar, but this scorpion and I are two of the creatures who helped to set you free aboard the boat that was taking you to the zoo. Do you remember?"

Eugene squinted, trying to see Bruce and the others through the mesh of the sack. "What are you doing here?"

"I might ask you the same thing," Bruce said, "but I'd rather do it outside of this sack, if you don't mind."

The weasel pulled at some bits of leaves and twigs that were stuck in his fur, but he didn't touch the bag. "I'm supposed to bring your bodies back, or at least parts of them. If I don't, I'll be in a lot of trouble."

"Who's making you do this?"

The weasel looked around, as if checking to be sure he wouldn't be overheard. "Do you know a salamander named Armand?"

Bruce became angry now that he was sure Armand was responsible for the bad things that had happened to him and his friends. "Yes, we know him. Is he the one?"

"Yes. I have to bring your bodies to prove you're dead. I'm going to drown you in the river."

Bruce shrank back in the net. He looked at the others trapped with him and pictured them being submerged in the river, struggling to get free, as the cold water surged around them, unable to breathe, until they died. His eyes lingered on Sam, on her beautiful wings and body, and he almost got sick, thinking how he couldn't stand to watch her die … couldn't stand to watch any of them die.

"Eugene, why are you doing this? Is Armand paying you? We can give you things—do things for you—remember, we set you free. Don't you owe us this much?"

The weasel regarded Bruce with a sour expression. "Armand pays me nothing."

Bruce thought that made no sense. "I don't understand. Why would you do something like this for nothing? For no reason?"

"Oh, there's a reason." The weasel's eyes hardened, and he frowned. "You left me and the other animals loose on the island, remember? I was fine there for a while, but later there wasn't much for me to eat, or at least nothing I could catch easily. I snuck aboard one of the boats going back to the mainland, and that's how I got to this lousy swamp.

Then I got stuck in some horrible green muck not far from here. I was sure I was going to die, but Armand and his rat saved me.

"At first, he said I owed him my life, and he just wanted me to do a few 'errands' as repayment. I thought that was okay, only I found out he wanted me to threaten creatures in the marsh so they would move away. He said it was all for a good cause. I didn't want to do what he asked, but he said if I didn't, he would find me, no matter where I went, and kill me. I believe him. Now he says I can buy my freedom by killing you and your friends. I don't have any choice. I want to be free, and the sooner I never see Armand again, the better. After I kill you, I'm going back for the rest of your friends."

Bruce's wings ached terribly, and it made it hard for him to think. There had to be a way to get Eugene to change his mind. What if Eugene brought their bodies back to Armand, and they looked dead but weren't really dead at all? Would Armand know the difference?

"Eugene—I have an idea. It will get you your freedom and my friends and I won't have to die. Will you listen?"

The weasel narrowed his eyes, but he agreed.

"Okay. This is what we'll do ..."

Chapter 28

Reunited

Bruce was glad when they neared the spot where they had been trapped and taken in the net, but his happiness faded when he saw Orville's unmoving body on the ground. He held onto the fur on Eugene's back, while Carly crawled down and surveyed the area to make sure it was safe. When she'd signaled it was okay, Angie and Sam flew toward Orville.

Out from the bushes beyond the path came Agatha, Milton, and Jemma, approaching warily, eyeing the weasel. Milton must have recognized Eugene, because he somersaulted, intending to land next to Bruce in their old game, but as he dropped, Milton tumbled to the side ungracefully—the first time Bruce had ever seen him miss a jump.

"Bruce, your wings! What happened?" Milton said, glancing at the others. "Are the rest of you all right?"

Bruce climbed onto Eugene's paw and held on while Eugene lowered him to the ground. "A rock hit Angie, too, but it looks like she's better off than Orville. Is he alive?"

Agatha nodded. "Alive, but barely. What happened to you, and who is your friend?" she said, motioning to Eugene.

"Agatha, Sam, Jemma—meet Eugene. The rest of you should remember him from the time we were on board the ship to the island. Agatha—you remember Lilly, the ferret who helped us while we were on the island? This is her brother."

"But isn't he the one who dragged you away?" Milton asked.

"Yes, but we struck a deal. Eugene is working for Armand, and he says it's Armand who is trying to have us killed. Eugene was supposed to drown us, then come back, get the rest of you, and take our bodies back to Armand to prove we're dead. I talked him into trying something different."

"Bruce, I think you could convince a dog to love cats," Milton said. "What's your idea?"

Bruce looked up at Agatha. "I heard my mother talk about some kind of herb or powder that makes creatures seem to be dead when they eat it, but they really aren't. Do you have any of that in your satchel?"

"If you're talking about wanting us to appear dead so that Armand will think we've been killed, I have one of the ingredients, but not the other."

Bruce's brow furrowed, and he tried to fold his wings without thinking, only to have pain shoot through them. He winced, and Milton came close again.

"We need to fix your wings before we go anywhere," Milton said. "I don't think you can fly like that."

Bruce shook his head. "Butterfly wings can't be fixed. Once they're broken, that's it."

Angie shook her head. "I don't think anyone's ever tried. The fact that butterflies can't fix their own wings doesn't mean that all of us together can't do something." She turned to Agatha. "Do you have anything—"

"I'm not quite sure what to suggest." Agatha moved closer to look at Bruce's bent and torn wings. "We can make a glue that might mend the one that's torn. For the other—we'd need to make a splint to hold it."

"I know!" Angie said. She flew back the way they'd come, dipped to the ground, and picked something up. When she returned, Bruce saw she was carrying a gray feather. "We can use a piece of this to be a stiffener," she said.

Agatha smiled. "Very clever, Angie. That should work nicely." She turned to Milton. "Would you bring my satchel, please?"

Milton's expression changed to one of dismay, but he walked toward the enormous bag. He took a deep breath and reached around it. With a grunt, he lifted the satchel over his head and stumbled forward. When he had almost reached Agatha, he dropped the satchel with a resounding thud. Everyone was startled and turned to look at him. He shrugged. "It was heavy," he said with a grin.

Agatha opened the satchel and took out containers of creams, powders, and other fluids, along with small bundles of dried pods and leaves which she set on the ground around the bag. "No, not those. Where are my … oh, there you are," she said, removing a small container made of a nutshell with another that fit over it for a lid. "This should do the trick. Carly—would you look through the stones nearby and bring me the flattest one you can find?" She passed the nutshell lid to Sam and said, "Please bring some water. Angie, would you pull one of the vanes from that feather and bring it to me? And Sam—would you find a small stick I can use to stir this up?"

Each of them went to do their assigned tasks. When Carly returned with a nice stone, Agatha poured a small pile of powder onto the flat surface. She took the stick from Sam and the container of water from Angie when she returned. Agatha poured a bit of the water onto the powder on the stone and mixed them together. It made a yellowish paste which she stirred into a goo. When it seemed completely mixed, she said, "Bruce, you'll need to hold very still, even if it hurts."

Bruce nodded, wondering how much it was going to hurt.

"Milton—I need you to hold his wing so it won't move. Can you do that?"

"Yes."

"All right. I'm going to put some of this mixture on the tear and see if we can glue it together again. Are you ready?"

Bruce nodded again, although he wasn't sure how much more pain he could stand.

Agatha dipped the stick into the mixture and held up a small amount. She touched the tip of the stick to the top of the tear, working the goo down the ripped area, smoothing it out with the tip of her other foreleg as she drew it along.

The mixture stung, and Bruce cried out, closing his eyes. The stinging got worse, and Bruce hissed.

"Don't move!" Milton said, holding Bruce's wing and wincing, too, knowing his friend was in pain.

Sam came forward and held Bruce's forefeet with both of hers. He opened his eyes and saw her close to him. He took a deep breath and held it, not wanting to appear weak in front of her. He vowed not to cry out again.

"There. That's done. Now we're going to work on the more difficult wing," she said, motioning for Angie to come forward. "Bring the vane." As Angie held it, Agatha dipped her stick into the goo again and spread it along the length of the vane. "Put the gooey part along the edge of the good part of Bruce's wing here, and hold it there" she said to Angie, pointing to where it should go.

Angie pressed the vane to Bruce's wing and held it there to stop the wing from moving. Bruce felt a searing pain along the edge of his wing where it had torn away. He tightened his muscles to counter the pain.

"Now I'm going to raise the bent part of your wing and glue it to the feather vane," Agatha said. "That will hurt, but I need you to hold very still. Milton, keep holding his wing to stop it from moving. Is everyone ready?"

Angie, Milton, and Bruce nodded, and Agatha lifted the bent portion of Bruce's wing and pressed it to the vane. Bruce shut his eyes again to help block the pain he felt. Agatha held the broken wing in place until the goo seemed to have hardened. "Angie and Milton, help me lower Bruce's wing to the ground so it lies flat. He should be more comfortable that way."

Bruce relaxed his wings as much as he could, considering the pain, and let his friends guide his wings down. When the wings lay flat, Bruce also flattened his body and lay unmoving.

"Bruce, I want you to stay that way as long as possible. It's important to make sure the glue is dry before you try to fly. I want to remain here for a while anyway. I'm hoping Orville may yet wake up and give us more information."

Chapter 29

Bruce and Sam

Bruce had been in the same position for so long that he was growing tired of holding still. He groaned and asked Agatha, "Do you think my wing is dry yet? My muscles are aching from not moving."

"Try lifting it now, but do it carefully. Start by bringing it up just a little. Let me watch as you do."

Everyone watched while Bruce raised his wings slowly. The injured wing stayed straight, and although it looked a little odd with the addition of the feather vane and the line of glue over the torn spot, it seemed to work well enough. "Oh, that's better!" he said, groaning. "I never knew doing nothing could be so difficult!"

Sam came close to Bruce and gently touched his forefoot with hers. "I'm glad it worked. I hope you can fly as well as ever. Maybe better!"

Bruce gazed at Sam and watched her antennas wave and wiggle. The light from the sun behind her created a glow around her head. He thought the soft fur around her eyes was beautiful. That same fuzzy feeling he used to get whenever Angie was around crept through his body. He recognized the feeling now and smiled. He wondered if Sam felt it, too.

"We've done what we can for you, Bruce," Agatha said. "Don't do too much too soon. Now I think it's time to concentrate on Orville. Would all of you—except Bruce, because I want your wings to dry a little longer—please take these containers to the river and fill them with water?"

The companions each took a nutshell and headed to the river's edge. When they returned, Agatha said, "I'm hoping the water may revive Orville. When I tell you, turn your container over and dump the water onto his head. Ready, set, go!" she said, and each of them dropped the water. Although the amount in each individual nutshell wasn't large, together the water made a decent splash, and it was enough, along with Agatha's prodding and pulling on Orville's paw, to cause him to rouse. Everyone moved back, giving him room to move.

"Mmph mrw rgh," Orville said, as he struggled to sit up, his pans and spoons clanking. He raised a paw to his head. "Oh, owww! What hit me?"

"That large rock there, I would think" Agatha said, pointing to the small boulder next to him on the ground. "Are you all right?"

"I don't feel good, that's sure. I can't quite see straight. Did someone attack me? Why would they do that?"

"I'm afraid it's probably our fault," Agatha said. "I think whoever killed Cecil wants us dead as well. You happened to be the largest target here."

Orville caught sight of Eugene. "Who's that? I've never seen a weasel around the marsh before."

"I'm not a weasel. Well, actually I am, but I prefer to be called a ferret, thank you. My name is Eugene."

"My mistake," Orville said. "I've only seen drawings of weasels. You're much better looking in person. Care to buy something? I have items for nearly everyone. Trinkets, beads, pots and pans, pretty—"

"Orville, there's no time for that now," Agatha said. "We need to get going, but we'd like to get back to what you were telling us before the rock laid you low. You were just about to tell us who the best suspect would be."

The woodchuck nodded, rattling his wares again. "Indeed." He looked at Agatha and his eyes lit up. "I don't suppose you have any more of those tasty tarts? I'm sure they would help me think much more clearly. If not, something else might do."

Agatha made a noise of displeasure, but she opened her satchel and produced two scones. "These will have to do. They're all I have."

The woodchuck took them and popped them into his mouth. His expression changed to one of bliss. When he'd finished chewing, he said, "I believe you must be the best cook in all of the marsh."

"That's been proven more than once," Agatha said, "but never mind. Back to the most likely suspect."

"Isabelle. I believe she killed Rodrigo, and I think she may be quite capable of committing such a murderous act again. What her reasons might be, I can't say. It's just a feeling I have."

"Orville—on a different subject: do you have any sleeping powder?"

The woodchuck's brow furrowed. "Hmm. I might. You can't sleep?"

Agatha shook her head. "It's not for me. Do you have enough to make all of *them* very sleepy?"

Orville reached into a bag he carried over his shoulders and pulled out a pouch. "This should be more than enough for your needs."

Agatha pulled an empty shell container from her satchel. "If you'd fill this, it should be plenty. What do you wish in return?"

Orville shook his head. "You watched over me when I was injured, and your wonderful cakes and tarts have my tongue smiling. You owe me nothing."

Agatha bowed to the woodchuck and took her full nutshell from Orville. "Thank you for your information and this powder. Now, if you'll excuse us, we need to get to work."

Agatha led the party a short way along the path, away from the woodchuck and began to pace. "Bruce's plan calls for the four original travelers—Carly, Milton, Bruce, and me—to appear dead when Eugene arrives at Armand's home. I'll mix the sleeping powder with an herb I have to make what's known as deathshade. Just before we arrive at Armand's, I'll mix the deathshade with water and have you drink it. Once you've gone to sleep, Eugene will carry you inside to Armand. Eugene, tell Armand that my body disappeared down river and you couldn't find it. Once Armand accepts that you're all dead, Eugene will tell him that his sister, Isabelle, wants to meet him at the bridge—that it's urgent. Once Armand leaves, Eugene will create a distraction for the guard and I'll sneak in and revive you."

She stopped pacing and turned toward the travelers. "It's important that you're revived before too long, or the deathshade could really kill you. With Eugene's help and good luck, everything will be fine. Once we're inside, we'll search for clues." She regarded her friends, one by one. "Are you willing to try this?"

Slowly, all of them nodded.

"Then let's go. We should get close to Armand's before nightfall and then get a good night's rest."

Chapter 30

The Sleeping Potion

Getting back to the area near Armand's home proved to be simple. Those who couldn't fly rode on Eugene's back. The ferret bounded through the forest and then the marsh, making excellent time, and they arrived before the sun had begun to set.

The evening passed quietly, except for the hooting of an owl that had them all, including Eugene, feeling nervous. They huddled close under cover of some leaves behind a rock. Agatha, Carly, and Angie formed one small group. Nearby, Milton and Jemma sat close to one another, and Bruce sat close to Sam a bit farther away. Sam sat on Bruce's good side, and he enjoyed the occasional moment when her wings brushed his as they fluttered.

He and Sam talked about where she grew up (not so far from Agatha's home), her family (lots of sisters and brothers and cousins), what she liked (nectar from honeysuckle) and didn't like (pollen from hibiscus flowers), and more. Bruce shared stories of his adventures with Milton and the others and how they got to be friends. By the end of the evening, Bruce felt as if he'd known Sam for a long time—as if they were old friends, too.

It was quite late when Agatha suggested they get some sleep. Bruce nestled against a tree, setting his wings upright, which seemed to be the most comfortable way to sleep. Bruce noticed Sam did the same, while Angie slept with her wings flat. *Must be one of the differences between butterflies and moths*, he thought.

He tried to sleep, but Bruce couldn't stop the thoughts of Sam circling in his mind, and later those were mixed with thoughts of what the morning would bring. He envisioned all of them lying motionless, as Eugene brought them in before Armand, who would look them over and dismiss them, and the ferret would take them away. These thoughts played over and over in his mind through the night, and when he woke in the morning, he felt more tired than when he went to sleep.

He noticed that Sam looked tired, too. In fact, everyone seemed apprehensive. He tried to dismiss the thoughts of what was to come and concentrated on paying attention to what Agatha was saying.

"... and try not to worry, as that never helps. Before I give any of you the potion, all of you need to crawl into Eugene's bag. Once you're there and settled, I'll give you the potion. Carly, since you're heaviest, you'll ride at the bottom of the sack."

Carly took that as a signal and crawled into the bag that Eugene held open for her. Angie followed, and she positioned herself on top of the scorpion, beneath her tail, so as to keep her wings as flat as possible and avoid having them damaged. Bruce followed, and he lay on his side next to Angie, his wings upright and flattened on top of one of hers. Milton came last, and he lay on the mesh next to the rest of them.

Agatha picked up the container with the potion she'd mixed just shortly before. She walked around the bag until she came to Bruce, who watched her from within the mesh. "You're first," Agatha said. "I want to see what happens as the potion begins to work. It's likely to affect you most, because you're the smallest, and I want to be sure you all wake up at the same time."

Bruce bristled. "I'm not the smallest. Milton is smaller than I am."

"Not in terms of body mass," Agatha said. "You have the smallest body, and you'll get a smaller dose. Still, I want to monitor the effect closely." She dipped a spoon into the container and brought out a small amount of liquid. "Drink this slowly," she said.

Bruce sipped the liquid, made a terrible face, pushed the spoon away. He coughed and nearly choked. "Aw, ack! It tastes awful!"

"I know it does," Agatha said, pushing the spoon toward him again, "but you need to drink it all.

Don't think about it. Swallow it quickly."

Bruce turned slightly green, but he drank the liquid, making horrible faces until it was gone. "That's the worst stuff I've ever tasted in my life!"

"Regardless of how it tastes, all of you need to drink it to make this work. Bruce, are you tired yet?"

"No," Bruce answered, but even as he said that, his head felt fuzzy, and he noticed the light fading. He decided it might be best to close his eyes. His head and feelers drooped.

"All right, he's asleep. Angie—you're next." Agatha held out her spoon and Angie echoed Bruce's faces of disgust at the taste of the liquid. As Milton swallowed, Angie was fading. When Milton's body drooped and his legs curled, Carly slurped the liquid.

"It doesn't taste *that* bad," she said. "I don't see what all the fuss was about."

"You just have a different constitution," Agatha said. "You and Milton are more alike than different. Carly—make sure you place your stinger outside the mesh so you can't sting anyone. Don't worry—I'll see you soon enough when you wake up."

As Carly's body started to sag, she wove her tail through the mesh with the stinger away from her friends. When all of the travelers in the bag were asleep, Agatha helped Eugene hoist the sack onto his back.

"Agatha, Jemma, Sam—come on. Time to go," he said. Once they were on his shoulders and had hold of his fur, he asked, "Ready?"

"Yes. Let's get this over with," Agatha said, and Eugene darted through the marsh toward Armand's home.

As Agatha spotted the guard in the path ahead, she whispered, "Don't forget to let us get off when you're past him. We'll meet you around back as planned."

Eugene slowed to a walk as he continued down the path. Agatha, Jemma, and Sam burrowed beneath the bag on his back and hoped the guard wouldn't take a close look. Eugene signaled to the crab as he approached. "Bringing these creatures to Armand," he said without stopping, and continued toward the entrance.

Chapter 31

Playing Dead

As Eugene neared the opening to Armand's home, Agatha crawled out from under the bag. She held the bag up so Jemma and Sam could get out, too. They scurried and flew to the back of the rock where they would wait for the ferret.

Eugene took a deep breath. "I hope this works," he said to himself as he entered the burrow. It was a tight fit, and he had to squeeze lower than usual to allow room for the bag on his back. Once he was inside, there was enough room for him to stand up and turn around, but that was it.

Armand didn't even turn at the sound of Eugene's entrance. "Is it done?" he asked, more concerned with what he was writing in his ledger than the ferret who dominated his living area.

"Yes." Eugene placed the bag on the floor, taking care not to hurt any of the sleeping bodies inside. "I drowned them all. The body of the mantis floated away, though, and disappeared down the river."

"You're sure she was dead?" Armand asked, raising his eyes to look at the ferret for the first time.

"Yes. I'm sure."

Armand stood then, working to straighten his bad leg, and limped past the mesh sack. He picked up a sharp wooden skewer from his cooking area. "I wouldn't want to find out you were lying to me," he said, as he fondled the skewer and made his way back to the sack. "Let's see if you're telling the truth."

He poked the sharp end of the skewer through the mesh of the bag and through both of Bruce's upper wings and one of Angie's before it hit the hard shell of the scorpion. Finding no response from the creatures, Armand smiled. He pulled the skewer out and brought the sharp end of it to his nose, savoring the aroma of the injury. "Well enough," he said. "You may go." Armand waved his paw toward the outside.

Eugene started to pick up the sack when Armand said, "Leave that here. I may have some use for their body parts."

Eugene looked dismayed. He started to leave, but turned back. "I almost forgot. I met Isabelle on my way here. She wanted you to meet her at the bridge as soon as possible. She said it was important."

A dark look crossed Armand's face. "What does she want?"

Eugene shrugged. "She didn't say. Just that she wanted you to come right away."

Armand muttered something Eugene couldn't make out and again motioned toward the opening. This time, Eugene turned and squeezed through the tunnel to the outside.

He checked that Kyle wasn't looking his way and walked around the back of the rock. "Agatha?" he whispered.

A voice from above said, "I'm here." Eugene looked up and saw Agatha, Sam, and Jemma in the tree overhead. The mantis opened her wings and dropped in front of the ferret. "Where are the others?" she said in a high voice.

Eugene squirmed. "Still inside. Armand said he could make use of their body parts." The ferret paused and said, "He stuck a skewer through the bag to make sure they were dead. I don't know if ..."

Sam gasped, and Agatha winced. "Is Armand going to meet his sister as planned?"

"I don't know. I told him she wanted him to come, but whether he'll go—"

"All right. We have to hope he will. If not, we'll figure out something else. Meanwhile, you need to go out front and keep that crab busy so we can sneak inside. Once I'm in, I'll give everyone the reviving potion while Jemma and Sam look around." Suddenly Agatha held her forefoot up and whispered, "Shh—I hear something."

They listened as Agatha moved ahead to peek around the rock. She saw Armand speaking with Kyle, who disappeared up the pathway as Armand went back inside.

"Go now," Agatha said to Eugene. "If the crab comes back, keep him busy, and sneeze loudly when it's safe for us to go in."

Eugene bounded around the rock and up the path to where the crab normally stayed.

Soon a large rat appeared, followed by Kyle, who walked to the opening of Armand's home. Moments later, Armand came out, and Kyle helped him climb onto the back of the rat. Once Armand was seated, the rat walked out of sight, apparently taking Armand to meet Isabelle. The crab headed back to his normal spot.

"Be ready now," Agatha said to Jemma and Sam. "We're waiting for Eugene's signal."

It seemed to take forever. Finally they heard some talking—it sounded like Eugene and Kyle—and a loud sneeze.

"Go!" Agatha said. She picked up her satchel and hurried around the rock, glancing up to make sure that Kyle was looking the other way. She hurried into the opening. Sam flew in next, followed by Jemma, who bounced off the walls on the way into Armand's home.

Agatha put her satchel down next to the mesh sack. She pointed to one side of the room and said, "Jemma, you start there." Pointing to the other side, she said, "Sam, over there. Look for papers or ledgers that might give clues about the blackmail or things involving Cecil."

Agatha looked through the mesh and saw the fresh wound the skewer had made in Bruce's top wings. She rummaged through her satchel and pulled out a different container of fluid and the spoon she used earlier. Carrying these with her, she opened the bag and crawled into it, taking care not to step on the occupants or get caught in the mesh herself.

She reached Bruce and dipped the spoon into the liquid, getting what she thought would be the right amount to revive him. She poured the fluid into her mouth and, holding it there, unrolled Bruce's tongue and took the end of it into her mouth as well. Using his tongue like a straw, she blew the fluid into him, hoping it would get inside to do the trick.

Nothing happened. She waited. Moments went by. She unrolled his tongue and blew into it again, hoping to force the fluid in farther. Still nothing.

Looking dismayed, Agatha decided to continue giving the fluid to the others. She again dipped the spoon, taking into her mouth a slightly larger amount of fluid for Angie. She repeated the process she'd used with Bruce, blowing the fluid into the moth's tongue.

Moving to Milton, she opened his mouth, took another spoonful of fluid, poured it in, and pushed his mouth closed. Agatha found the most difficult task with Carly, since it was nearly impossible to get her mouth open. She finally managed it and poured a large amount of the liquid into the scorpion.

Someone stirred. Seeing Angie's wings fluttering slightly, Agatha scurried out of the bag.

As Angie woke, she groaned and cried out. Her eyes opened. She looked around and then at her wing. "Oh, no," she cried, still groggy from the sleeping powder. "What happened?"

"Your wing has been injured, but if you can manage it, come out of the bag now, before the others wake up."

Agatha held the bag open. Angie crawled over Carly until she emerged from the mesh, her injured wing dragging at her side.

Milton woke next, and Agatha coaxed him out of the bag, followed by Carly, who seemed more alert. Finally Bruce began to move, and he winced when he roused a little more and his wings moved. Agatha noticed that both Sam and Jemma now stood near the opening of the bag, waiting for their friends to emerge.

"Bruce, your wings have been injured again," Agatha said, and he nodded, holding the pain inside and saying nothing. Agatha turned to her helpers. "Did you find anything?"

Jemma shook her head. Sam did, too, and said, "Nothing. He doesn't have any papers or books."

Agatha looked puzzled and cocked her head.

"Keep looking. I'm sure he has some, but he may keep them hidden. Look for secret hiding places behind or inside of other things."

Both of them seemed unhappy at having to leave their friends, but they did as Agatha asked and began searching again.

"Angie, Bruce—I'll repair your wings later. For now, I'd like to help the others search. The sooner we find what we came for, the better."

Milton stood and said, "I can help look, too." He wobbled a bit, but he managed to walk toward Jemma, who was scanning inside the fireplace.

"So will I," Carly said, and she moved toward Sam, who was searching under a table.

As Agatha began to search, Bruce said, "Look under the rug. When we were here before, I noticed that Armand always walked around it, even though going over it would have been the shortest route."

Agatha walked to the rug and pulled a corner of it back, revealing a large hole.

"That's it!" Agatha said, and she pulled the rug back farther. All the friends, including Bruce and Angie, who appeared to be making the best of their wounds, moved closer to peer into the hole in Armand's floor.

Chapter 32

Evidence Found

A ramp led downward. Carly moved onto the ramp, taking the lead. "Stay here," she said. "I'll let you know what I see."

The scorpion scuttled down and out of sight.

A few moments later, she called, "Come on down. I think what we're looking for will be here."

Agatha started down but then stopped and turned around. "One of you should stay here and alert us if you hear anyone coming back. Who has the best hearing?"

They looked at each other, and Angie said, "I think I do."

"Okay. Keep listening outside. If you hear anything, call out."

Agatha went down the ramp and the rest followed. Carly stood in the center of a large room. Two walls had shelves containing baskets and bundles of goods. Some of the baskets held fur, feathers, roots, and pretty rocks. There were also containers of liquids, powders, and dried fruits and seeds. On either side of the entrance were more shelves which held books and ledgers, and against the last wall was a writing desk covered with piles of papers and writing implements. To the left of the desk was another opening in the wall.

"Ah! This is what we're looking for, I think," Agatha said. "I'll check the desk. Spread out and look on the shelves and in the books for clues. Carly—would you look down this passage," she said, pointing to the new opening, "and tell me where it goes?"

Carly headed to the opening.

Everyone was quiet as they searched the shelves. Agatha shuffled through the papers and read one of the ledgers on Armand's desk.

"This ledger is a record of the "gifts" Armand received from his various sources," Agatha said. "He is getting payments from someone named Ruth, someone else named Stephen, and— "

After a pause, Sam asked, "And what, Agatha?"

Agatha looked up. "Not what, but who. Armand is blackmailing his own sister, Isabelle."

A long silence ensued. "Does it say what she did that she doesn't want anyone to know?" Sam asked.

"No, but I can guess. Has anyone found anything else?"

"Nothing," Jemma and Milton said together.

"Just ordinary stuff," Sam said.

"I've found the eggs Horace was bringing to Armand before," Jemma said, pointing to one the baskets.

Agatha closed the ledger and scanned some of the other papers on Armand's desk, and then she opened the single drawer. Inside were more papers, along with a small bottle that seemed to be made of bone. It was ivory colored, and it looked very old. Carved along the side of the bottle were the initials "I. M." Agatha pulled the stopper and sniffed the contents. Her eyes went wide. "I've found a small vial of peanut oil," she said, "and the initials on the side of the vial are 'I. M.'" Agatha's eyes were steely. "It doesn't prove that Isabelle is the killer, but I'd call it a piece of evidence that can't be ignored." Agatha replaced the stopper and put the bottle into her satchel.

"I've found some more letters," Milton said. He turned one over to see how it was signed. "Love, Isabelle," he read. He turned the letter over again and read it aloud.

'Armand—You must help me. Someone is threatening me with blackmail over Rodrigo's death. Yesterday I received a letter saying whoever sent this knew I killed Rodrigo and where and when. The writing isn't familiar to me, but they're demanding I gather mushrooms and deliver them to the bridge by sundown tomorrow. I'm not to stay there—the note says if they find me there, or if I don't make the delivery, this creature, whoever he is, will tell all. I'll comply this time, but what's to stop him from doing this again? I've told no one but you, but now someone else has found out. Can you help me, dear brother?'

"Poor Isabelle," Agatha said. "She doesn't realize the brother she's confiding in and asking for help is the one who is using her so badly."

She glanced at Bruce, who hadn't moved from where he stood at the bottom of the ramp. "Bruce—why don't you take the letters back upstairs and put them into your notebook. We'll be up shortly."

Bruce started up the ramp just as Jemma said, "Here's a basket of yellow flowers," holding it so Agatha could see inside. "Are these the flowers Rodrigo used in his stew?"

Agatha hurried over. "Yes, Jemma. They are." She looked pained. "While it's possible that Armand discovered the location of the flowers himself, it's much more likely that whoever killed Rodrigo learned where they are and is now delivering 'gifts' of flowers to Armand." She began to say something else when she heard Angie call, "Stay there! Someone's coming!"

Chapter 33

Brother and Sister

Angie and Bruce hurried to the rug, pushed it back over the opening, and moved behind the couch to hide. Bruce watched as Armand walked in and sat down in a chair. He wasn't limping. *Perhaps his injury is an act,* he thought. *If so, then his alibi is no good, and he could have murdered Cecil.*

Another salamander entered, this one using a cane, and Bruce realized the first salamander must be Isabelle, Armand's sister.

Bruce's heart was beating fast as he looked to the rug on the floor. Angie had hollered for the others to stay below, but did they hear her?

"What's this?" Isabelle said, pointing to the empty mesh bag on the floor.

Armand's expression grew dark. "Kyle! Come here!"

Moments later, the crab poked his head inside the opening. "Yes, sir?"

"Did you see Eugene? Was he carrying some bugs' bodies?"

"I talked with Eugene after you left, but I didn't see any bugs."

"Find Eugene and bring him to me. Oh, and take this with you," Armand said, pointing to the empty bag on the floor.

The crab took the bag and left. Isabelle stood and strolled to the cooking area, where she picked up some of the eggs Armand kept for a snack. Munching these, she said, "Something missing? Who are these 'bugs' you're looking for? Are they a problem?"

"The problem isn't the creatures, Isabelle. The problem is *you* and the messes you keep getting into."

"I just need you to help me figure out who is blackmailing me. You have spies everywhere. It should be easy for you to do this for your only sister."

"I don't care about your blackmail, Isabelle. What I *do* care about is that a group of creatures is traveling around the marsh asking questions about Cecil's death. Sooner or later, if I don't stop them, they're going to figure it out. That should concern you more than being blackmailed."

"Even if they find out, they can't prove anything. Even with proof—what of it? Oh, yes—I'll be turned out of the community. Considering that I've been shunned since Rodrigo's death, it's not much of a worry, is it? Even though no one could prove I killed him, everyone assumed I did. Now no one but you and that trader—what's his name? Orville?—will have anything to do with me. These bugs aren't going to kill me, are they? They wouldn't dare—not with you as my protector."

Bruce couldn't stand it anymore. He walked around the couch and said, "Isabelle, your brother isn't protecting you. He's the one you should be afraid of. *He's* the one who's blackmailing you."

Both salamanders stared at Bruce, and Isabelle's eyes grew wide as she considered this possibility, but her expression returned to one of nonchalance. "He wouldn't do that. Not my brother. Armand—who is this butterfly? Is he one of the bugs you're looking for?"

"Kyle!" yelled Armand. "Come here!"

"Yes, and so am I," Angie said, as she leaped from her hiding place behind the chair. "Before you ignore what my friend is saying, consider that we have proof your brother has been collecting goods from his blackmail of you. See for yourself. Look down below in his secret room."

"Kyle! Where are you?" Armand yelled more loudly than before.

Carly entered Armand's room from outside. "Kyle won't be coming," she said. "He's a bit 'tied up' at the moment." She walked backward toward the opening and said, "If you would be good enough to follow me ..." Then she turned and walked outside.

"Armand, who are these creatures? What are they talking about?"

"Nothing, Isabelle! They're spewing nonsense."

"But they're talking about the blackmail. How could they know about that?"

"They've obviously been searching around here. They probably found your letter asking me about it." Armand picked up his cane and headed toward the opening.

"You're not going after them, are you?" Isabelle asked.

"I'm going to get this over with," Armand said, as he disappeared outside.

Isabelle heaved a great sigh as she followed him, saying, "Why can't you just help me and ignore these creatures?"

Bruce was the last to go outside, and he stayed close to Angie on a rock just beyond the opening.

Kyle, the crab, was tied up with cords. Orville was there, too. He was also tied up, and his containers and tools lay in a pile on the ground. Eugene stood next to a medium-sized rat. Closer to Armand were Agatha and the rest of the friends Bruce thought were still underground inside Armand's house. Even Horace was there, flitting from one place to another overhead. Where did Orville and Horace come from?" Bruce whispered to Angie. "How did Agatha and the others get out here?"

Angie only shook her head and shrugged her shoulders.

Chapter 34

The Fight

Armand shielded his eyes as he surveyed the creatures outside. Isabelle moved up close behind him.

"Armand, what's going on?" she said.

"My question exactly." Looking at Agatha, he said, "What is this about?"

The mantis strode closer. "We know you've been blackmailing residents of the swamp, including your own sister. We found your record books and we saw the many 'gifts' so conveniently left for you by those residents and retrieved by Horace and this rat.

"We found a flask of peanut oil bearing the initials I. M. We know that peanut oil killed Cecil, and it's hard to come by around here. Of course, when you have a trader who is working with you and your sister, providing the ingredients you needed to commit a murder—well, things become simpler."

Armand waved his cane and shook his head, as if to dismiss Agatha's words. "This is foolishness. You can't prove a word of it."

Isabelle moved out from behind Armand and stared at him. "I never understood how anyone could have found out about my stealing Rodrigo's recipe. You were the only one I told, the only one who could possibly have known, yet I kept thinking someone else must have discovered it, because my brother—my only brother—would never tell anyone. It was unthinkable that he would do such a thing. But now—they say it was *you* who has been blacking mailing me? *You?*"

"Stop this nonsense, Isabelle. Don't listen to these idiots."

Agatha waved her forefoot. "When you and your sister were on your way back here, you didn't realize we'd come out of the back exit from your underground cellar. We followed you and listened to your conversation. It was very enlightening, especially the part about how you had a rat put the stone in front of Cecil's home, and when that didn't work, how you had Eugene 'kill' us, so we wouldn't be snooping around anymore."

"*These* are the creatures who've been asking all the questions?" Isabelle said. "That means what they're saying is true. You *have* been blackmailing me! My own brother!"

Isabelle leaped on top of Armand and they both fell to the ground. She bit him on the neck behind his head, and the two of them struggled, as Armand tried to get free. They squirmed and circled on the ground, but she held on. Suddenly, he was loose and he leaped at her, but with his bad leg, he couldn't make a proper jump. She bit him again, this time on the throat, and blood flowed down around his body and onto the ground. Armand pulled at Isabelle and pushed her body with his feet until he managed to break free again. This time he bit her, and Bruce heard bones snap in her foreleg.

The fight became frenzied. No one tried to stop it. Bruce watched, transfixed, as the ground became more and more bloody, and great open gashes appeared on their necks. Soon it was hard to tell which of them was which, as they circled and flipped each other over in the mud. One of them lost a foreleg completely—it jiggled on its own in the mud—and when one bit the face of the other, Bruce wondered if its eyes were lost as well. The fight continued, with one salamander rising to the top, only to have the other gain ground and overcome the first, in a reverse of positions.

Finally, Armand and Isabelle's circling became more labored. Their sides heaved in and out very quickly, and Bruce could hear their heavy breathing, panting like dogs. After one more tangle of legs and teeth, the two lay on the ground, one over the other. Bruce thought Armand had the better position, but he wasn't sure. They lay that way, with the jaws of the one on top biting the one on the bottom, for a long time, until the one on top let go and moved, collapsing a short distance away. Both salamanders had their eyes closed.

The onlookers didn't go near them for a long time. They stood, rooted, unable to believe the spectacle they'd just seen.

Finally Carly moved closer to the salamander Bruce thought was Armand. "Are you alive?" she asked.

There was a long pause and a labored breath. Armand opened his eyes, "Yes, but not for long, I think," he said, his voice barely above a whisper. He opened his eyes. "Is she dead?"

Agatha moved close to Isabelle's body, touched her side, and listened. She nodded.

"Yes," Carly said.

Armand sighed again. "She and I—it shouldn't have ended this way."

Agatha walked to Armand. "You must have known she would find out one day."

The salamander coughed, and blood seeped out through his mouth. Bruce thought Armand was right and he would not live much longer. "Did you kill Cecil?" he asked.

There was a long pause, and Bruce wasn't sure Armand was still breathing, but finally he answered. "I guess it doesn't matter now if you know all of it." He took a deep breath and continued, his voice very soft now. "No, that was Isabelle's doing. She took some of my peanut oil and put it into Cecil's stew."

Agatha moved closer to the salamander and leaned down near him. She was shaking. "Did you kill Rodrigo?"

"No, Agatha." He sighed. "It was Isabelle. Always Isabelle."

The salamander convulsed in pain, and Agatha moved back, giving him room. Bruce could see tears on Agatha's cheeks.

Armand coughed. "Isabelle was infatuated with Rodrigo—she emulated him and wanted him to care for her." Armand closed his eyes, as his body spasmed in another wave of pain. "Isabelle followed him when he went to gather his yellow flowers. She confronted him and told him of her love. No doubt he told her he loved you, and she couldn't stand that. She told me she pushed him under the water and held him there until he stopped moving."

Armand convulsed once more, and then he stopped breathing.

Chapter 35

Case Solved

The travelers sat in Horace's home, listening to the rain pour outside. Agatha had a number of things cooking, and she'd brought out all the goodies remaining in her satchel for the group to eat until her meal was done.

Like the others, Bruce was somber, reflecting on what had happened that day and the loss of two more lives. Yet, the search for information was over, and they'd achieved what they set out to do: find Cecil's murderer. That gave Bruce some satisfaction, even though he now had patches on all but one wing and a fair amount of pain to show for the ordeal.

Sam snuggled closer to him, and he felt suddenly warm again. He was glad she hadn't been injured on this journey. She was as beautiful as ever, and he still couldn't believe she was interested in him and had decided to travel with him on his way home.

His gaze traveled to Milton, who sat paired with Jemma, the two of them playing some game that required one of them to pin the other's leg. It looked like they were weaving invisible webs together. The smiles on their faces meant they were happy, and that's all that mattered.

Bruce's eyes found Angie sitting with Horace and Agatha near the cooking area. Agatha had done a good job of mending Angie's wing, making the repair almost invisible. Angie said it didn't hurt anymore, and Bruce was glad. His injuries still bothered him, but he wouldn't let on.

"We'll let that simmer for a while," Agatha said, as she sat close to Angie. "Oh, my feet ache," she said, massaging each foot in turn.

Silence settled over the room. Bruce was tired, and he assumed everyone else felt the same. It was hard not to think about all that had happened, though, and he found himself trying to fit the pieces of the puzzle together. He was thinking this might be a good time to ask Agatha about some of his remaining questions, when Angie spoke first.

"Agatha, you talked with Kyle, the crab bodyguard, and Orville and the others after … after it was all over. Why was Armand blackmailing those creatures?"

Agatha continued rubbing her feet. "We already knew that Armand had Horace delivering notes to various creatures demanding payment. Horace also picked up the deliveries those creatures made, leaving them in a different place each time, where one of Armand's rat friends would pick them up and bring them back to Armand. I can't say *why* he did it except to get more goods that he could trade with Orville and to become richer."

"Is Orville a bad guy?"

"I'll let you decide that. Orville did some bad things. He admitted that he and Armand worked together to recycle the goods Armand got by blackmail. Let's take Isabelle, for example. She would drop off mushrooms for Armand, who would sell them to Orville, who would trade them to the next creature needing mushrooms to satisfy Armand's blackmail request. Everyone made out well that way—except the creature being blackmailed."

"Why did Orville come to Armand's home?" Bruce asked.

"He said he wanted to warn Armand that we were close to figuring out what they were doing. He couldn't do that because we got there first."

Milton stood up, stretched, and said, "Did we ever find out why Armand wanted to own all the land in the marsh?"

Agatha nodded. "Yes. The rat explained that. Evidently the rats used to live here long ago. At that time, the land was dry, and the river didn't flow here. Then men built a dam that diverted the water to this area and flooded the marsh.

"The rats were unhappy, as they kept their goods and treasures buried, and now they couldn't retrieve them from under all the water. They moved to higher ground beyond the river and made an agreement with the beavers to divert the water back again. However, the beavers were only able to do so much, and the marsh became what you see today. Even now, the rats can't retrieve their treasure because of the green moss."

"So Armand was going to help them?" Jemma said.

"In a way. Armand had many connections throughout the area, and he and the rats and the beavers came to another agreement to build a canal that would drain the water out of the marsh, allowing it to dry up. Once it was dry, the rats would dig up their long-lost treasure, Armand would get part of it, as would the beavers, and the rats would go back to living on the high ground."

"But the rest of the creatures in the marsh—the creatures who need it to be wet to survive—what about them?" Sam asked.

Agatha shook her head. "They'd be forced to move," she said. "Armand's efforts to get the marsh creatures to leave were just a way of getting them to do something they'd be forced to do eventually."

Milton asked, "Did Armand send the magpie to warn us away? And the rat with the rock at Cecil's home?"

Agatha let the foot she'd been massaging drop to the ground. "Yes. Armand assumed we might find out about Isabelle. Even though he was blackmailing her, he still loved her and evidently didn't want to have her secrets brought out into the open."

After a moment of silence, Bruce asked, "Agatha, did you ever find out why Isabelle killed Cecil?"

Agatha was silent for a long time. "Yes, Bruce. It was a mistake."

Bruce couldn't believe what he'd heard. A flurry of chatter started, as the friends tried to make sense of what Agatha had said.

"What I should have said is that Isabelle meant to kill Cecil, but her reason for it was a mistake. The rat told me Isabelle made only one payment of goods to Armand before she asked him to find out who was blackmailing her. Little did she know it was Armand himself! Anyway, Armand sent her away without help, and she decided to act on her own. She dropped off spices at the prearranged location. Then she circled around and hid where she could see who picked them up. Horace arrived and took the spices, so she assumed the blackmailer was Cecil, since Horace worked for him. That also made sense because Cecil was researching the marsh. She probably thought Cecil had found her out." Agatha stood and walked toward her satchel.

"Agatha—"

"The rest of your questions will have to wait until tomorrow. I need to get back to my students. We can talk more as we head home. Besides, as I understand it, someone here has a ceremony to plan." Agatha smiled, and Angie blushed so her fur turned pink.

Chapter 36

Going Home

The seven of them made an interesting sight as they made their way back to Agatha's. They walked and flew slowly, taking time to rest often. Besides wanting Bruce and Angie's wings to have more time to heal, Agatha said she knew they still had questions that needed answers before they could put the journey to rest, so a slower journey would give them more time to talk.

Bruce rode on Carly's back, and Agatha carried Angie. Milton carried Agatha's satchel, which was much lighter than it had been, yet Milton moaned often about why he'd gotten stuck with it and why Carly couldn't carry it instead.

"If I took the satchel, you wouldn't have anything to complain about," Carly said, smiling at Milton. "Besides, it will build up your muscles. I'm sure female spiders appreciate muscular mates."

Milton sputtered and started to reply, when Jemma said, "Oh, we do. Perhaps he needs some help?" She did a somersault in the air, landed next to Milton, and raised two of her legs to help him carry the bag. Milton pulled the satchel away, lost his balance, and tumbled sideways. The satchel landed with a thud on the ground. Everyone laughed. Milton tried to look upset, but he started giggling, and soon everyone was completely silly with laughter.

"It's good to laugh after such a serious time," Agatha said. "I'm certainly glad you two found each other."

"We are, too," Jemma said, still giggling.

"And Bruce—you and Sam seem to be getting along well," Agatha said.

Sam nodded, and Bruce blushed when everyone grinned at him. "Bruce and I were talking about that. Even though you all came to the marsh for a sad reason, good things came from it. If you hadn't come, I wouldn't have met Bruce, and Jemma wouldn't have met Milton."

"Coming to the marsh did something else—something very important for me," Agatha said. "Along with discovering who killed Cecil, we solved the mystery of Rodrigo's death. I have carried that with me for a long time, and now my mind can rest. I miss him still, but at least I know what happened."

"Agatha—do you think you'll ever find another mate?" Angie asked.

"Hmph," Agatha said, turning her head and stopping in her tracks. "I'm probably too old to think about that now—although, I suppose, if the right mantis happened to come by ..." She smiled and started walking again.

Everyone was silent for a while. Finally Angie said, "Carly, you never talked about your plans for mating."

Carly flicked her tail and continued walking. "That's because I don't have any. As Agatha said, if the right scorpion came along ..." She paused. "I wasn't going to say anything, but there was a point on the trip where I felt jealous of most of you. You all had someone—Agatha, even you had loved Rodrigo—and I've never had anyone who wanted to mate with me. I talked myself out of those feelings, but they happened." She paused. "If I'm not mistaken, some of you have felt that way, too."

Bruce looked uncomfortable. He knew Carly was talking about him. He figured if he didn't answer, the conversation might change, so he stayed quiet. He was surprised when Angie spoke.

"I felt jealous when Sam came along and Bruce went to talk to her. It didn't matter that Tom is waiting for me at home. I didn't want to lose my friendship with you, Bruce. I don't feel that way now that I know Sam better, because I know you and I will always be friends. I hope you'll come to my mating ceremony, Bruce. In fact, I hope *all* of you will come."

Everyone nodded and said they would be there.

Bruce was silent a little longer. Finally he said, "Milton, I was jealous of Jemma when she stayed with you in the marsh. I couldn't figure out why I felt that way until Carly said I was afraid of losing you as a friend. But it was more than that. I didn't want to share you with anyone. I also didn't want anything to change."

"Yet you were ready for a change when you found Sam," Carly said.

Bruce blushed again, but he nodded. "You're right. Guess I've been kinda selfish."

"Humph," Carly said. "Change is part of life. Things don't stay the same forever. If they did, we'd never grow up or learn new things or meet new creatures. When things are good, we want them to stay the same. When things are bad, we want them to change. And sometimes, when change happens, we aren't ready for it. In the end, we're all selfish when it comes to change."

"Well, I'm certainly ready for a change of who's carrying this satchel," Milton said, dropping the bag on the ground with a thud. "Bruce, you're kind of fat, but how about trading places?"

"Kind of *fat?*" Bruce said, as he climbed down from Carly's back. "The only thing fat around here is your head."

"Do they always do this?" Jemma asked Angie.

"Always," Angie said, smiling. "Always."

Chapter 37

Friends

Bruce was getting tired and his mother, Arlene, was panting a little as they flew. They'd had to stop when a flock of birds flew close and landed in the tree where they'd hidden themselves among the leaves. When the birds finally left, they had to hurry, knowing it wouldn't do for one of the new chefs to be late to her first day of school.

"I wish we'd left sooner. You never know when something like this is going to happen," Arlene said, looking fretful. She had made a backpack for herself to go with the one Bruce usually carried, and both were full with spices, herbs, extracts, oils, and other ingredients she thought she might need. "Is it much farther?"

"No, we're almost there. In fact, I can see it now. See that big rock? It's right there."

As the two of them flew closer, Bruce saw Milton and Jemma playing outside, jumping from place to place. He called to them, and they waved.

When Bruce and his mother reached the entrance to what had been Armand's home, they touched down and walked inside. The home had been converted to a cooking school. The main room was equipped with several cooking stations, each with a set of pots, pans, and cooking tools. Around the outside of the room were shelves with bins of specialty items. Bruce thought this was a wonderful use of the home that would otherwise have been empty now that Armand was gone.

"Arlene!" Agatha said from across the room. "I thought perhaps you'd decided not to come. I'm so glad you didn't change your mind."

"No, I didn't change my mind. I'm as eager as ever to become a chef. Just that some birds decided to camp out where we were hiding."

"Well, get settled at your station," Agatha said, waving toward one at the end. "We're going to have the dedication soon."

Bruce looked around. "Are Angie and Tom here?"

"Yes—I think they're down below. That's where we're gathering for the ceremony. Where's Sam?"

"She'll be along. She had to go home for something."

"That's right—she lives near my old home, doesn't she?" Then Agatha's expression changed and she smiled, tipping her head to one side. "Have the two of you decided to stay together?"

Bruce blushed. "I think so. My parents like her, and I'll be visiting her family when we leave here." His antennas twirled a little as he said, "If it all works out, Sam and I will be looking for a new home together soon." Agatha returned his smile, and Bruce headed down the ramp that had been widened leading to the space below. This room had been converted to a lecture and study area. Shelves with cookbooks lined the walls. Today the "Thornberry-Moss Chef's Academy" would open its doors. Bruce and the rest of his companions had journeyed back to the marsh once more to celebrate the school's dedication to Cecil and to congratulate Agatha, who had returned to live in the marsh and become its headmistress.

A large pedestal stood near the front of the room where the dedication would take place, and Bruce saw Angie and Tom standing near it reading the inscription. He walked toward them and smiled. It was hard to believe so much time had passed already since their time here in the marsh. Angie and Tom's mating ceremony had taken place soon after they returned, and Bruce and the others had all been there, enjoying the rituals of dance and flight. Despite his expectation that he wouldn't like Angie's new friend, Bruce found he couldn't help but enjoy Tom's company, and he understood why Angie loved him so much. Milton and Jemma had traveled to visit her parents and had remained there until this ceremony could take place. When it was over, they planned to travel to the island to visit Milton's home and receive his family's blessing on their mating.

It had all happened so fast. One moment, he'd been a young caterpillar, dealing with bullying at school. Then he'd gone on an adventure and learned the value of real friends. He'd found the courage to stand up for himself and those he loved. He'd learned that those who love and cherish you are your *real* family, and that included his parents, as well as Milton, Angie, Carly, Agatha, and now Sam and the others. His family had grown quite large.

Coming here, he'd learned again that most creatures are neither all good or all bad. On his last adventure, with Carly's help, he'd realized that even *he* wasn't above lying when it suited his purposes or if he felt it was justified. Here, while searching for Cecil's murderer, he'd learned about blackmail, jealousy, and greed, and he realized that, despite how grown up he felt now, he still had much to learn.

He thought about Agatha's question about Sam. He loved her—that much he knew for certain. It helped that she was pretty, but he'd come to love much more about her: the way her antennas wiggled when she was happy, and how much she seemed to care for him, too. But was he ready to leave his family and join with her and then to mate and have caterpillars of their own?

His reverie ended when he heard a voice behind him call his name. He turned to see Sam flutter down the ramp. She was radiant, even in the low light of the room. His heart beat faster, and he could only smile as she flew to him, touched her forefeet to his, and nuzzled the side of his head with hers. He flushed and knew that she was meant for him.

"Milton and Jemma are coming, and Carly, too."

"Attention, everyone," Agatha said, stepping toward the pedestal at the front of the room. "It's nearly time to start. Please take your seats and we'll begin."

Bruce and Sam sat next to Angie and Tom, and Milton and Jemma sat on the other side of Bruce, who looked around for his mother and Carly and saw them coming with the others who began taking seats. Bruce also recognized Cecil's brother, Frederick, and his daughter, Polly, as well as several of Cecil's students and their parents.

"Please take your seats, everyone," Agatha said, beaming at the crowd. When everyone had quieted down, she continued, "Cecil would have been so honored by your presence here. I, too, am honored to lead this school and share the knowledge of fine cooking with those who would aspire to be chefs." Agatha waved one foreleg in a circle, indicating the room around her. "The recent days have been a difficult time, with the sadness following the loss of Cecil and the difficult effort of tracking down his murderer. However, good things often accompany the bad, and the use we are making of this building is evidence of that. I hereby dedicate this school to the memory of Cecil

Thornberry, the first Master Chef, for his efforts to share his love of cooking with his students."

Everyone cheered.

"Now, before we starve, let's get to the long-awaited student cooking competition! Students—to your stations. Start cooking!"

Bruce's mother hurried toward the ramp, along with the other students, and Bruce motioned for Carly to join him and his companions. She made her way past those heading upward. It was clear that many of them had never seen a scorpion up close before, and they kept their distance, despite the pact of safety at this event.

Bruce thought again that Carly was now the only one of his companions who didn't have a mate or someone who would be soon. He wondered if she felt alone in their company now. He decided to say something, hoping to make her feel better.

"Carly, I wanted to let you know that … that I know you'll find someone soon, someone who'll mate with you. In the meantime, you'll always be one of *us*."

The scorpion smiled. "There's no need to try and make me feel better when I feel fine," she said. "I'm quite content. Besides, I *do* have you as my friends, and you're all the family I need right now. When I decide it's time to mate, the right scorpion will come along, and I'll bring all my babies by to torment you.

Bruce smiled. "Will they be as horrible as you were?"

"*More* horrible," Carly said, winking. She glanced at Agatha, who was talking with Frederick and Polly. Waving a claw in their direction, she said, "I wouldn't be surprised if Frederick falls for her. He's been ogling her all afternoon."

Bruce watched Agatha and realized she was unaware of Frederick's obvious overtures. "Looks like you may be right," he said. "That could be a nice thing." He turned back to Carly. "Well, whenever it happens, I know you'll be a great mom," he said.

Carly blushed—the first time Bruce had ever seen her do that. He reached forward and touched her claw. "I'm glad we found you."

Smiling, she said, "I am, too." With that, Carly turned and walked up the ramp.

The rest of the group stood in a circle looking at one another.

"It's strange how you never know what's going to happen," Angie said.

Bruce thought about that. He never could have predicted any of the things that had happened to him, and he wondered what the future would hold. His friends were going their own ways now, and that was both sad and happy at the same time. *Things change,* he thought, *whether you want them to or not. The only thing to do was to take what came and try your best to be a good mate, a good son, and a good friend.* A twinkle came to Bruce's eye, and he smiled. *And to hope there will always be a new adventure.*

Books by
Gale Leach

The Bruce and Friends Series:

Bruce and the Road to Courage

Bruce and the Road to Honesty

Bruce and the Road to Justice

Bruce and the Mystery in the Marsh

Other Books:

The Art of Pickleball

Visit **www.galeleach.com** to learn more about these books and others in the works, and sign up to receive my newsletter and blog posts by email.

Facebook: https://www.facebook.com/GaleLeachAuthor

Gale Leach lives in Surprise, Arizona,
with her husband, three cats, and two dogs.